GRAVITY CHANGES

BOA wishes to acknowledge the generosity of the following
40 for 40 Major Gift Donors

Lannan Foundation
Gouvernet Arts Fund
Angela Bonazinga & Catherine Lewis
Boo Poulin

GRAVITY CHANGES

STORIES BY ZACH POWERS

American Reader Series, No. 27

BOA Editions, Ltd. ❖ Rochester, NY ❖ 2017

Manufactured in the United States of America

First Edition
17 18 19 20 7 6 5 4 3 2 1

For information about permission to reuse any material from this book, please contact The Permissions Company at www.permissionscompany.com or e-mail permdude@gmail.com.

Publications by BOA Editions, Ltd.—a not-for-profit corporation under section 501 (c) (3) of the United States Internal Revenue Code—are made possible with funds from a variety of sources, including public funds from the Literature Program of the National Endowment for the Arts; the New York State Council on the Arts, a state agency; and the County of Monroe, NY. Private funding sources include the Lannan Foundation for support of the Lannan Translations Selection Series; the Max and Marian Farash Charitable Foundation; the Mary S. Mulligan Charitable Trust; the Rochester AreaCommunity Foundation; the Steeple-Jack Fund; the Ames-Amzalak Memorial Trust in memory of Henry Ames, Semon Amzalak, and Dan Amzalak; and contributions from many individuals nationwide. See Colophon on page 176 for special individual acknowledgments.

Cover Design: Sandy Knight
Cover Art: *Invisible Cities* by Matt Kish
Interior Design and Composition: Richard Foerster
Manufacturing: McNaughton & Gunn
BOA Logo: Mirko

Library of Congress Cataloging-in-Publication Data

Names: Powers, Zach, 1980– author.
Title: Gravity changes / Zach Powers.
Description: First edition. | Rochester, NY : BOA Editions Ltd., 2017. |
Series: American readers series ; 27
Identifiers: LCCN 2016051932 | ISBN 9781942683377 (paperback)
Subjects: LCSH: Imaginary places—Fiction. | BISAC: FICTION / Short Stories (single author). | FICTION / Fantasy / Contemporary. | GSAFD: Fantasy fiction.
Classification: LCC PS3616.O94 .A6 2017 | DDC 813/.6—dc23
LC record available at https://lccn.loc.gov/2016051932

BOA Editions, Ltd.
250 North Goodman Street, Suite 306
Rochester, NY 14607
www.boaeditions.org
A. Poulin, Jr., Founder (1938–1996)

In memory of Jeremy Mullins,
who knew most of these stories before they were written,
and to whom I owe an eternal debt.

Contents

Gravity Changes

When I was a boy we walked on walls. The kids these days climb trees like it's some sort of accomplishment. Look how high they go. How high! Nervous mothers look up at them and urge care, or coax them down with cookies to the flat, flat ground. Play in the mud and dirty your clothes, children. Press flat. Stay low.

I'm no physicist, so I can't explain it. Gravity just worked different back then. I walked on the ground, came to a wall, and kept walking right up it. Oh, how I remember eaves and overhangs! Dangling upside down with the sidewalk overhead. We didn't think of up and down, though. The ground was something different, we knew that, but down denotes the pull of gravity, and with the pull so uncertain we had no word to describe it.

In summer I would stand on the brick wall of the old bank building and drop a ball to my best friend who stood on the wall across the street. I say drop because, once released, the ball would fall away from me without propulsion. It simply fell, like it knew in which direction I wanted gravity to pull it. My friend would drop the ball from his side and it would fall back to me. Sometimes another friend would pass on the street below. We would drop the ball to him, and he, in turn, would drop it back to one of us. In the middle of the game one day, I missed the ball. It struck the wall and bounced off at a crazy angle, darting around in open space, like a hovering fly, until it finally fell to the ground and bounced to a halt.

From this, we first conceived the idea of flying. It was a simple act of will. I shouldn't say simple. There were many bruises and busted noses as we perfected the process. Was it rightly flying? I don't think so, not by the standards we have today, when flying is a fight against the concept of down, but we didn't have that concept back then. In reality, we were falling, which I guess is the opposite of flying. But if you fall in one direction just a little faster than you're falling in the other direction, then you can glide through the air, suspended between the warring tugs.

At first, we fell too fast, a dozen boys tumbling through the open space above Main Street. My best friend broke an arm on his initial attempt, falling uncontrolled from one wall to another and smacking with a gross crack against the orange bricks, just missing a window, which surely would have cut him all to hell. There were tears in his eyes but he wasn't crying. He looked up at the wall he'd fallen from like it was a thing he didn't understand. When he came back from the hospital his arm was encased in a bright white cast, which we all signed, and then he walked to the center of the wall and tried to fly again. He came back from the hospital a second time with a cast on his other arm, and we signed that one, too. Before he could try another flight his mother showed up. She took his hand and pulled him from the wall to the ground and led him away down the sidewalk. He was forced to stay in his room for the rest of the summer, pacing the floor, the walls, the ceiling.

By this point, a number of us had achieved our first jerky flights between buildings. The first time I flew it was like the opposite of a bouncing ball. I floated away from the wall, mere inches, then fell back. I floated a little farther, then fell back. Twice as far still, and then back. After a number of these inverse bounces, I reached the middle, dead center between the two walls. I fell back once more, and with a grin I'm sure was wide (missing, at the time, one baby tooth knocked out in a previous failed flight attempt), I pushed off and sailed across the expanse. As I neared the other side, I slowed myself, beckoning to the gravity of the other wall, and landed with just a tap of my toes against the brick.

The other boys cheered and laughed and smacked each other on the back. So much laughing! Even a few adults, watching from the street, clapped their approval. The adrenalin of success pumping through me, I pushed off again, reached the middle, that beautiful point of no return, and I stopped. I floated there. I spun myself, arms spread wide, above me the sky and below me the ground and vice versa. I list that moment with my wedding and the birth of my children as the happiest of my life. In fact, at the wedding, after kissing my bride, I stepped back and spread my arms and recreated that twirling triumph, this time on the ground, which by then had in fact become down and inescapable. I didn't think it sad then, but looking back perhaps it was a dark gesture, though I'd intended exuberance. I'd intended nothing at all.

For the rest of the summer we floated between buildings, above the ground. Seldom in the city did we walk. Flying became natural. While our parents had been skeptical after our initial injuries, they warmed to the practice, and eventually praised us for our grace. A few parents even joined in, but remained awkward in that way adults are when taking on something new so late in life. My own father tried to fly, but he never managed to get more than a few inches off the wall.

School began again in September. We returned to the tight hallways, where we floated from class to class. But as the year wore on, routine pressed down upon us and soon enough we were walking like everyone else. Outside the air grew colder, and the naked space between the flat walls seemed inhospitable. Only sometimes, in a moment of whimsy, would one of us rise from a wall, usually the old bank building, which somehow felt more solid than all the rest, and float against the biting winds that pushed harder than gravity pulled.

Even as the air warmed, we walked like everyone else. The heat hunched us over like something we carried on our backs. It was the first time I ever noticed the drops of sweat running down my face. I think we were still able to fly. It just never crossed our minds to make the attempt. Looking back, I'm not sure if it was the heat making us feel heavy, or our own heaviness that made us feel the heat.

In the sky, in our place, floated a group of boys too young the year before to participate. It was them turning in the air, gliding from point to point. Gliding to nowhere in particular. We looked up, not with envy, but with regret. That's the only thing left when you land.

Slowly, without anyone noticing, without comment, we abandoned even the walls and walked only on the ground. The walls became something new, defined in terms different from the sidewalk. Even before gravity changed, our perception of the world had changed as if to accommodate what was to come. I remember the first time I went around a building instead of over it. It was the old bank, its walls a place I'd walked since

I could remember. But that day, to even think of walking up it felt like effort. I turned and followed the sidewalk beside the wall, dragging my fingers across the brick. I wasn't the only one grounded. My friends were right there with me, funneling through the streets of the city. We looked up from the ground at the new generation of flying children. Free, so free! And still we didn't join them.

I came home from college, dressed in my school colors, and found the town I had left strangely flat. The walls still stood tall as ever, but I saw them as walls. In my education I had learned the word *down*, and my feet treated the concept as law. With each step, I reiterated my orientation. My legs felt heavy. Too heavy. I grew weary and leaned against the wall of the old bank. The brick pressed into my cheek, rough and wonderful. I pushed my palm into the surface, felt the skin take on the inverse of the jagged texture. So heavy! I sank to the ground, sat back against my beloved wall.

Above me I saw the current generation of flying children. One little girl was teaching herself how to fly, never venturing far from the wall from which she had launched, all the time looking up at her bolder friends. I felt lighter just watching them. They glided, as I once had. I remembered games played weightless in empty space. We'd swoop down on the girls and flip the backs of their skirts over their heads. We'd jump from the roofs of buildings and turn somersaults in the air, perform loops and cartwheels. We'd tie streamers to our feet, pretending to be kites.

I pushed against the ground, lifted myself up with difficulty.

I don't know why, but that's when it changed. That's when gravity turned into what we know it as today. Down transformed from a concept to a fact, perpendicular became an impediment, and flight became impossible. I realized it, somewhere inside, even before the screaming.

The children fell from the sky. Dozens of them. I ran to where they were falling, I guess to try to catch them. They fell too fast. Their little throats screamed such high sweet notes that I cried even though the meaning of what was happening hadn't sunk in. The screams stopped short with a series of noises I won't relate, because I don't have the language or the desire to relate them. Little bodies dotted the street, and the first of many mothers wailed. This new scream was deep and throaty and echoed between the walls.

The little body nearest me was mine. It felt like mine. I saw myself, the boy that I had been, dead on the street on the ground I'd once thought conquered. I felt nothing but a curious detachment. Had I a stick, I would have poked the body.

More parents screaming. Sirens in the distance, getting closer.

Below these louder sounds, I heard a whimper coming from above me. The little girl I'd noticed earlier hung from the gutter of the old bank. Her fingertips clutched the sharp edge of the metal, knuckles buckling under the unidirectional pull of this new gravity. I ran beneath her. Fall, I yelled. Come down. She looked at me, shook her head. It's just like flying, I said. Let go and I'll catch you. She shook her head again, but at the same moment her little fingers, bloody and tired, gave out and she fell. Down she came. She landed in my arms, and the weight of her knocked me to the ground. My head smacked against the pavement. Stars danced in the bright blue of the afternoon sky. The clouds remained aloft.

⁂

The whole town crowded into the cemetery. One by one the little caskets were lowered, down past the level of the ground.

I saw some of my old friends among the mourners. We didn't speak to each other. I think we felt guilty. It was our summer of flight, which seemed impossibly long ago, that had led in the end to this. I comfort myself with the fact that everything ends with a funeral.

The little girl, the one I'd caught, huddled close to the thigh of her father, pigtails bouncing whenever she moved.

How pigtails give me hope. How they resist the pull of gravity.

A Tinkle Is the Sound of Two Things Meeting but Failing to Merge

No. 1

The girl was born with the head of a boy growing out of her right shoulder. As she reached adolescence, when she showered or changed her clothes, the eyes of the boy would look down at her growing womanliness with desire and sadness. He desired to touch what he saw, but they weren't his hands to which he was attached. Or if they were his hands then so too were they his breasts, his triangular tuft of hair, and his loose skin between the legs he could sometimes catch a glimpse of in the mirror. Maybe the other head was the intruder.

Eventually the girl took to touching herself, and the boy felt nothing through the hands, nothing from between the legs, and he knew for sure none of it was his. The girl, sensing his sadness, or growing tired of her fingers and hoping to experience the coupling she heard the single-headed girls talk about, decided to act. She went to the garage and took an old wood saw from the pegboard. She sawed away at the base of the boy's neck. There was no pain, except once when she cut too close and nicked her shoulder.

A small flap of skin remained connecting them, but it couldn't bear the weight of the boy's head, which tottered, ripped off, and fell to the concrete floor. The boy winced at the impact, but was grateful to settle at such an angle that he could look up at the girl and admire the even shape of her shoulders.

No. 2

The husband sat on the couch every day, and at night he fell asleep there. He ate his meals from the coffee table, and though he must have gone to the bathroom on occasion, his wife never saw him rise from the cushions. Always in the background the television cackled, and he stared at the screen without ever focusing on the pictures. The husband grew heavier from eating bad food and never moving. With each day he sank deeper into the cushions until the wife said she could no longer tell him apart from the couch, or the couch from him, for the essence of each had seeped into the other. Where once rested the couch and on the couch rested the husband, there was now a blob of unidentifiable material, neither man nor couch, but at once vaguely mannish and couch-like.

The wife hosted a cocktail party one evening. The guests could locate only limited seating, unable to discern the couch from its occupant, and when the husband greeted them, they did not know the source of his voice.

"What was that?"

"That's just my husband."

"But where is he?"

"He's there on the couch."

"What couch?"

"Bah," said the husband, and he stood up.

The guests gasped. To them, he had suddenly appeared out of ambiguity into concrete form, and behind him the couch had similarly emerged.

The wife turned around to find she could no longer recognize her husband or the couch and perceived only empty space where they had been.

No. 3

They clinked the wine glasses together. Then again. They clinked harder and harder until they finally clinked so hard the glasses shattered. With new glasses they repeated the process. Again the glasses shattered and the cascading shards embedded in the flesh of their hands. Blood dripped onto the starched white tablecloth and blended with spilt Merlot. They tried all night, went through dozens of glasses, but no matter how hard and earnest their toast, the glasses cracked. They were left with topless stems held in the tips of their pallid, red-streaked fingers.

"To the future," they said, thinking of a future where the two glasses were one, sipped at from opposite sides by each of them. The distinct properties of the individual glasses would give way to a unified whole, the original components forgotten. Pushed together like two lumps of clay, leaving only a larger lump identified without reference to any preceding lumps or other subdivisions, down to the molecular, to the subatomic. But first, a toast.

Again the glasses shattered, and, giving up, the couple turned to their entrées, which were long since cold and covered with glass.

No. 4

"I painted these paintings for you."

"I don't like them."

No. 5

When he retired the old man built a boat. He went to the forest and cut down the trees for the wood. He shaped the trees into planks and beams. He nailed and bound and glued them. Once the shape of the hull was formed he sealed it and painted it white. Along the top he painted a red stripe. He removed the branches and smoothed the trunk of the thickest tree. He mounted it in the middle and secured to it a white sail that would seem to glow in the sunlight. He mounted the rudder from brass fittings. He carved oars in case the wind wasn't blowing.

The sun was bright and the wind strong on the day he loaded the boat onto its trailer and took it to the lake. There had never been a boat more boat-like. As he backed down the boat ramp the other boaters stopped to stare. With wonderment they beheld the white sailboat with the red stripe and the sail that looked like glowing silk. From the top of the strong mast to the lowest protrusion of the rudder, nothing had ever represented the idea of a boat more perfectly.

The old man felt the weight of the boat float away, and he pulled his truck forward, dragging the trailer out of the water. He parked and returned to his boat at the end of the boat ramp. He stopped. The boat was not floating in the water as he had thought, but hovered in the air two feet above the lake.

The old man's old fishing buddy walked over.

"That's truly a fine boat," said the old friend.

The old man shook his head. "But how can something so perfectly formed fail to do the thing it is perfectly formed to do?"

"You'll catch plenty of fish in that old girl."

But as the old friend said this the boat floated higher. It drifted in front of the sun and never emerged from the glare.

No. 6

The little girl peered from around the door, which was open just enough to see out into the yard. In the yard the little girl's best friend was playing with an imaginary friend. The best friend's imaginary friend was an imaginary version of the little girl. The best friend saw the little girl in the doorway and waved. Suddenly ignored, the imaginary friend disappeared. The little girl closed the door slowly, peeking out the whole time. The door was fully shut. The best friend climbed the climbing tree in the yard, all the way to the top, and stayed there forever.

Joan Plays Power Ballads with Slightly Revised Lyrics

Joan shrinks the universe.

She types on her laptop, poking at the keys. An open copy of *Swann's Way* rests beside the computer, spine broken, the glue of the binding crumbling. She transcribes the text verbatim. Verbatim until page 372, where she changes one word. She types the rest of the book out as is. She saves the file, closes it, opens a new one. The white of the virtual paper fills the screen. She flips back to the first page of the Proust. She types again, from the beginning, everything in the book. This time she changes a different word. She has done well over five hundred one-word revisions of the novel.

I once tried to read *Swann's Way*, but didn't make it past the first chapter. Joan's persistence impresses me. It's why I love her, even if I don't understand. Love is a difficult concept. Given to subtleties and vagueness. Impenetrable and impervious to even the most determined probes. Poking at love like her fingers on the keyboard. A poke for each letter, space and punctuation in the book, multiplied by five hundred. And she hasn't even started the other volumes. Still, love survives.

I ask her for the five hundredth time why she makes so many revisions of *Swann's Way*. She pauses in her typing.

Even though she is impossibly persistent, I know her fingers grow tired. When we walk in the evening, my hand does all the holding. Hers rests limp in mine, trembling slightly. The tremble is almost imperceptible, like the subtleties of love. Only knowable as an uneasiness in the stomach.

She looks up from the pages of the book. Her eyes struggle to focus.

"I'm shrinking the universe," she says.

"How does that work, again?"

"The most detailed way to describe something is in terms of everything that it's not. An object is defined by the sum of its absences. The universe, the collection of all objects, is the inverse of the sum of all the objects that do not exist. It's what's left when you remove the near-infinite unrealized variations of everything that does exist, the permutations and misprints and could-have-beens that never were. It's a sculpture chiseled from an impossibly large stone, and all the leftover chips and chunks, flakes and flecks, define the shape of what remains. The more pieces left out of the universe, the more terms there are to define it from the perspective of what it isn't. The definition of the universe is bigger when there are more nonexistent objects by which we can, through an inverse procedure, describe it."

I nod. "So by creating variations of Proust, you're decreasing the number of nonexistent objects and thereby decreasing the size of the universe as described by the nonexistent."

"Shrinking the universe. Halting its expansion. Keeping our neighbors close."

"Close enough for what?"

"For camaraderie. For friendship."

"For love."

She removes her tired fingers from the keyboard and strokes the hair on the back of my head. I think of the individual follicles, all different, millions of them, but still just a tiny fraction of what could be. I lean forward and kiss her lightly on the mouth. I try to kiss her differently each time. Sometimes long and deep, sometimes just a brush of the lips. Otherwise I'm scared she'll get bored. Or the distance between us will grow as the universe expands us apart. Can I kiss her often enough, with enough variety, to maintain our closeness?

Every morning I wake up with my arms extended, reaching, having dreamt of her falling away, of our portions of the universe hurtling apart. In the dream I knit sweaters and fire pottery and fold swans of different papers, but no act of creation is enough. I lack her patience and her courage. I wish Joan would win the fight, halt the universe, so that I could sleep and feel love unaccompanied by worry.

❖ ❖ ❖

Worry is a complicated thing, full of variations and subtlety. Forever shifting and unsure. That's why it's worrisome. Unknowable, like an all-inclusive universe, with nothing on the outside to define it. If everything existed we would all be still, with no room to move. Not even to wiggle. Maybe a subtle vibration of the firmament, agitated by our worry.

We are mailing a postcard to Joan's mother. The front of the card depicts the Eiffel Tower. The scene is in the evening, when the framework of the tower shows as a black fractal against the tangerine sky. Wispy clouds hover in the background, indigo. The blinking red light on the top of the tower is frozen on, lit forever in the photograph. The back of the card depicts whiteness and a place for the address and a copyright in French.

We drop the postcard into a mailbox on a street in Kalamazoo, Michigan. We have mailed 720 identical postcards to Joan's mother from mailboxes across the country. Each postcard perfectly identical except for the postmark, changing to represent whatever municipality in which we find ourselves. Across the whiteness of each card Joan writes *Wish You Were Here! Love, Joan*. Each time she writes the phrase exactly the same, stroke for stroke, down to the smudge where she drags her pinky through the still-wet ink. The skin of her knuckle soaks up the blackness and no amount of scrubbing gets it clean.

Joan says instead of the unread revisions of books, postcards at least reach an audience of one. She says it's a matter of meaning. Can a book that no one reads really be called a book? Even a short message, once read, has more meaning than a thousand unread pages of manuscript. So she's moved on from writing books, limiting herself to this single line. I don't know if anyone reads the postcards, but I affix the stamps just the same.

Joan's mother died in 1982.

Wish you were here.

⁘ ⁘ ⁘

We are pretending to shop for a new car. We are perfectly happy with our current car, but pretending to be car shopping allows us to wander the dealership without suspicion. A salesman approaches us. I step forward to meet him, shielding Joan from his view. I talk with him about gas mileage and horsepower and side impact safety ratings. He tells me of resale values and J.D. Power initial quality awards. We talk about the American car industry. He's from Detroit, he says. That's where they make cars, he says, but in his eyes I see reflected the charcoal husks of dead factories, and lines of foreign-made cars fleeing the withered city.

Behind me, Joan walks down the row of shiny new cars. Their windshields are painted with prices and discounts and APRs. Balloons are tied to radio antennas. Little plastic flags snap in the wind.

Joan carries a key jutting out from between the first two knuckles of her left hand. Her pinky knuckle is still black with ink.

She circles a car, inspecting it closely. Despite our ruse, the inspection is sincere. She is looking for something. And when she finds the perfect spot, she jabs the key into the clearcoat finish, digs down to raw metal. She gives each car a small ding, each in a different location, to mark as unique the otherwise sameness of midsize sedans. She distinguishes, beyond color and optional features, each boxy SUV from the next.

We reach the end of the row, far away from the showroom. The salesman is still with me, discussing payment plans and financing options.

Joan stops and says, "We'll take this one."

She gestures to a bright red sports car. The salesman trots back to the showroom to get the paperwork ready. He just needs us to sign on the line, he says. It'll take him five minutes, he says.

Once his back is turned, before he's even halfway to the showroom, we leave the lot. The salesman will search and search for us, his commission, but all he'll find is a series of random dings in the smooth finish of the merchandise.

❖ ❖ ❖

But I'm confused by the car dealership. I'm unsure of our mission there. It seems different from Joan's past efforts. I ask her how come we damaged the cars. It seems less like an act of creation and more like an act of differentiation. We didn't add anything to the universe, merely altering what was already there. And since cars are all subtly different from each other, imperfections in the plastic and the metal and the glass, then all she did was add another, purely cosmetic, difference to the already differentiated.

Joan rests her head in my lap on the sofa. She smiles and strokes my arm. Her fingers feel strong. For the first time in a long time her touch is not lethargic. She commands her muscles and they obey and her fingertips tickle the thin skin on the back of my hand. This is part of her answer to my questions. She needs a vacation, her fingers say. All those creations, the thousands of retyped novels, the looping script on a thousand postcards, every repainting of the *Mona Lisa* with every imaginable variation of eyebrows—all these acts of creation are a drain on her hands.

Joan speaks, this time with her mouth.

"It's the same mission, scratching the cars, but a different method. Creation is probably best, but it's not the only way to shrink the definition of the universe. If you can make an object easier to describe, then it can be identified in fewer words, or in the case of the universe, transcendent of language, simpler to conceptualize. Before they were damaged, the appearance of each sedan was insufficient to identify it, so that a description had to begin with inconsistencies introduced in the manufacturing process. It's difficult, for example, to tell you how to pick out the car with the metallurgic defect in the engine block. It's difficult to describe a metallurgic defect at all. On the other hand, it's considerably simpler to tell you to find the car with the two-millimeter ding a centimeter below the left taillight. It's a conceptually simple differentiation, and therefore simplifies the definition. If I asked you to describe a person to me, probably the first detail you would tell me is the sex of the individual in question, thereby eliminating about half of all possible people. A difference in sex is obvious and easily observable. If instead you described to me someone by their heart rate, I'd have to understand the complex inner workings of their circulatory system for your description to be useful. At least I'd have to check their pulse. The process of understanding an individual as such would be made more difficult.

"So I've made each of those cars easier to identify, which is the same thing as making them easier to define. Fewer words, a smaller concept, to describe what is basically the same item.

"And my hands feel better today than they have in years."

To illustrate this last point, she unbuttons my shirt, top to bottom, fingers nimble, sliding down effortlessly as if operating a zipper.

⁘ ⁘ ⁘

She finishes undressing me, making quick work of my undershirt, my pants, my boxers. Using only her fingers she brings me to climax. As my panting fades she strokes my chest and my stomach, her face close to my ear, breathing lightly. She strokes lower, and, feeling that I'm ready to go again, stands up to remove her own clothes.

Usually I undress her myself, but I want to let her fingers do everything. They brush across the cotton of her shirt, the silk of her bra, the leather of her belt. Her fingers, so active, caressing, searching. I gaze at them, twigs with knots for knuckles, aged decades more than the rest of her from constant use, but just then looking young and beautiful again, like how they would look if she'd never become aware of the universe fleeing her, threatening to escape her eager grasp.

She grasps me, almost too hard, pulls me close. We kiss. I kiss her firmly at first, then lap at her lip with my tongue. She giggles, and I imagine her as a younger version of the woman she is now.

She pushes me away and climbs onto the sofa, positioning herself upside down, back on the seat, legs extended up the backrest. She shifts until her crotch is at the same height as the back of the sofa and motions me over. I climb up, struggling to position myself above her. My knees rest on the sofa table, hurting already, and I lean forward, hands on the edge of the coffee table. I squirm back and forth until my appropriate parts are aligned with her appropriate parts.

It isn't our most creative coupling, but this one is different, which, as always, is the only important criterion. I guess there are two other criteria, each marked by a groan and a quiver, a spasm and a sigh, and I'm glad to say, more often than not, all three criteria are met.

I never call the act making love, since with Joan it's as much a technical achievement as it is a physical extension of the emotional. Each time it's something new. A new pose, a new contortion. But maybe it's more like love than the endless repetition of the missionary position. Always the awkward unfamiliarity of new lovers.

We rest on the couch, oriented rightwards. I wrap my arms around her, clasp my hands to her hands, interlocking. Her fingers fidget. Restless. Unused to this excess of energy.

⁂ ⁂ ⁂

Joan expands her audience.

A new drummer takes the stage behind her. He is the sixth different drummer of the concert. The other musicians in her band trade out every few hours, guitarists and bassists with fresh fingers. Like the band, the audience changes. The door is a constant bottleneck of newcomers and departers. Those on the way out sweaty and drunk, those coming in heading in that direction.

I cough. Cigarette smoke clouds the air, barely overpowering the scent of stale, spilt beer and body odor. My cough can't be heard over the sound of Joan's band. I'm pretty sure I have permanent hearing damage. I've been listening to Joan's first set for the last thirty-six hours. She strums unerringly away at the guitar and belts out the lyrics to power ballads. She is currently singing her twenty-seventh consecutive rendition of Slaughter's "Fly to the Angels." Each time she sings different lyrics. Just a word or two. Changing the meaning of a line or a verse. Making the song, not really her own, but entering it into the public domain of the universe.

One of the roadies scampers out on stage and squirts water from a bottle into Joan's mouth during an instrumental interlude. I don't think it's enough water to replace the sweat she's dripping. Her top hangs low, the neckline sinking, soaked through. Her hair is completely matted, sticking in clumps to her face. She stares intently at the microphone in front of her.

I decide that this is the masochistic version of "Fly to the Angels." Joan tweaks the lyrics so that it's an epic ballad to the love of pain. Oh, the pain, the pain. Her guitar pick is worn down to almost nothing. The fingers of her left hand bleed, worn raw against the strings. The dirty burgundy of dried blood cakes beneath her nails. Still she strums, unaware or uncaring.

She sings the loudest part of the song. Her voice gurgles, vocal chords exhausted. The melody is lost in the gurgling. She gurgles louder to compensate. Louder. She stops singing. Her eyes roll, head lolls back, knees buckle. She collapses onto the stage, fingertips smearing four lines of blood onto the worn hardwood.

The crowd cheers as if this is all a part of the show. And maybe it is.

⁂ ⁂ ⁂

I wrap Joan's bloodied fingers in cocktail napkins and carry her outside. The taxi driver helps me get her into the backseat. He makes a joke about drinking too much. I make a joke about singing too much, doing everything too much, but he doesn't understand. I wonder if I understand it myself. Don't let her throw up in the cab, the driver says. Fortunately, he says nothing about dripping blood on the upholstery.

On the ride home I direct the driver to cut down side streets, double back, take the expressway, take back roads, follow that car, stop for gas, turn left on red, roll through stop signs in neighborhoods that aren't mine. Finally, I tell him to stop in front of our building. Even though she's asleep, I think Joan appreciates the route. We've never come home this way before.

The driver and I lift Joan out of the back seat. I lean her against the cab as I pay the fare plus fifty percent. With her limp body balanced on my shoulder I climb the stairs to our apartment. Inside, I peel off her matted clothes, wipe her down with a washcloth, and run a brush through her hair. I rub antibacterial cream onto the tips of her fingers. She tries to say something as I set her into bed, but it comes out as a gurgle. Her eyes slit open. She reaches up and touches my face, leaving a smear of the cream on my stubbled cheek.

I have never before seen her so tired.

She sleeps.

⁂ ⁂ ⁂

When I wake up in the morning Joan is on the couch watching TV. I have never seen her watch TV before. The sound is turned down, or maybe my ears have yet to recover from the concert. She has strapped Band-Aids over her fingertips. It makes her look amphibian, like the bulbs on the toes of a tree frog.

Still not fully awake, I flop down next to her. What are we going to do today, I ask. She bought a sewing machine last week and I'm eager to see what she makes with it.

Her eyes are glazed, fixed on the TV.

I touch her cheek. She smiles. The expression doesn't imply happiness. Then is it a smile? A new expression created just now on the sofa.

Joan shuts off the TV, but she keeps staring at the vanished picture. She speaks, not necessarily to me.

"I've never really considered anything else, content to make my tiny additions to the universe. But maybe it's not the best way. Maybe a single act of creation can be greater than the sum of everything I've done before. It's not a question of quantity, but one of meaning. The more meaning I introduce into the universe, the less non-meaning there is outside it. Each creation has depth, and revisions of books and songs and paintings are shallow compared to the originals. When I think of it, I've barely shrunk the universe at all."

I put my hand on the back of hers. She recoils slightly, but lets me keep it there.

"I'm done," she says, "making things with my hands. When I got dizzy on the stage last night I knew what I had to do. The room swirled around me, and I felt it swirling inside me."

She moves my hand to her stomach.

"I'm pregnant."

I look at her fingers, already still, retired from the act of creation. Her eyes, unfocused, remain directed at the darkened television. I lift her hand and kiss it. I get up. I go to the kitchen to make breakfast. Joan stays motionless on the sofa.

A shrinking universe inside her.

Children in Alaska

She glowed Easter yellow in the charcoal grays of the kitchen. *I'll be right back*, she said, descending into the pitch black of the basement where the spiders and the roaches live because they are averse to even the faint glow from the windows. I don't worry about her in the dark, though, because she is a lightbulb. Not a regular lightbulb, but one the size of a person. Five-feet-four from her cap to the crown of her bulb. Her filament dangles provocatively, a thin white fissure behind the frosted glass. Her breath is the faintest hum of electrical current. At night I dream of sleeping beneath thick black power lines, and old black crows come there to perch, and with them I listen to the humming.

Hello mother, I said, *this is my new girlfriend. Do not be alarmed, she is a lightbulb.*

I can see that, said my mother, always kind and understanding.

When we were married, very few people came to the wedding, and the kiss was awkward. At the reception I noticed several lightbulbs who had not attended the ceremony. They hovered near the bar, accepting new drinks as soon as the old ones were empty. I never mentioned this to my wife because I did not want to upset her, but in every other way I have always been perfectly honest.

Are you ashamed of me, she asked one night. *You never take me anywhere.*

No, I am not ashamed of you, I said, *but you do not fit in the car.*

We walked to the lake and circled it on a path carved into the underbrush mostly by joggers, but also sometimes by couples like us, or by people walking dogs. Darkness was setting in, but the path ahead was illuminated by my wife's face, so we walked well past nightfall and the fireflies swarmed around us. The waters of the lake splashed on the bank and old toads croaked to each other from opposite shores. We stopped in a clearing beside the path. My wife dimmed her light and we made love. Dry leaves rasped against her glass. Her buzzing came louder and at a higher pitch. I could not hear the toads anymore.

The pregnancy ended in miscarriage after only one month. When I cried to the doctor, *Why us why us*, he said, *Probably because lightbulbs weren't designed for birthing.*

We bought a dog. This was not to fill our childless void, but for the same reason that anyone buys a dog, though that reason is not clear to me. We named him Sparky, and Sparky would prance around us or lie in the corner by the heat vent. Sparky loved my wife. He would curl next to her in our bed and his golden fur would blaze with reflected light. One day we were walking Sparky around the lake, near the spot where once my wife and I made love. Sparky dashed into the lake and swam far out into the middle where his head was just a small dome on the water. He went under and we never saw Sparky again. I knew that he drowned, but my wife believed he lived on in the lake. She had never swum there, could never know anything but the unbroken surface.

I crashed the car. My wife rushed into the hospital, humming frantically, barely able to articulate the simple question *Where is my husband?* I was in a full-body cast in the ICU, watching reruns on the wall-mounted television. My wife flickered as she wept at the sight of me, which must have been rather pathetic, and I wanted to hug her but could not because my arms were encased in plaster.

We took the insurance money and bought a van. The back doors opened wide enough for my wife to fit inside. How long had it been since we'd last been on a date? Not since before we were married, when I had the pickup truck, and she rode in the bed, and in my rearview mirror the world looked bright and alive behind me.

We went to the movies. The moviegoers around us whispered through the previews until one of them left and returned with an usher.

The usher said, *I'm sorry but your light is washing out the screen.*

That is no light, I said, *that's my wife.*

The usher laughed and walked away. He left us standing in the middle of the aisle. My wife blushed, casting the red of her face over everything in the theater.

We went to bed without speaking. Faint bursts of light flashed from under the covers with each of my wife's sobs. I wanted to comfort her, but I didn't know what to say. I never know what to say.

Maybe we should take a vacation, I said, so we packed the van and rode northwest through all those middle states with interchangeable names, across the border into Canada, all the way up to Alaska. We stopped in Dogpatch, north of Fairbanks, because the name reminded my wife of Sparky, and for the first time in a long time warmth returned to her glow.

It was dark the day we arrived. And the next day, and the day after that. We walked down the street and my wife looked bright as the sun in all that darkness. Several of the local children began following us. Bundled in thick jackets and bulky boots, they moved like astronauts, crunching the snow with each step. They let my wife's light fall across their faces, then scampered away, laughing into the dark. By the last day of the trip, two dozen children followed us everywhere we went.

Our van pulled away and in the mirror I saw all their sad young faces peeking out from hooded jackets.

I could stay here forever, my wife said.

I didn't have the heart to tell her that the days would last as long as the nights.

My wife descended the stairs into the basement. The doorway grew darker. I poured myself a glass of water and sipped it, thinking all the things one does when met with a moment of quiet. The noise came from far away. It was a mere tinkling, faint and forgettable.

I looked down the steps. Blackness, like the long Alaska night. No matter how much I strained my eyes I couldn't see anything. Where was the flashlight? When had I needed a flashlight in all my years of marriage? I threw open drawers in the kitchen and found it buried beneath rubber bands and twist ties. I flipped it on. Descending the stairs, I paused on each step, sweeping the weak beam in front of me. There was the faint scent of hot metal. At the bottom I felt for the light switch.

A naked bulb, like a toy version of my wife, swung from a cord attached to the ceiling. Shadows swayed back and forth. All across the floor, shards of frosted glass glinted in the dim light. My wife. What was left of her. I picked up the nearest fragment, a triangle just large enough to show the curve of the glass, and turned it in my hand. The raw edge sliced my finger. Blood filled the line of the wound and flowed out onto my skin. I let the shard slip to the floor.

The broom. The broom was in the kitchen.

The Eating Habits of Famous Actors

All the main characters are dead now. I am afraid I'm all you have left. You probably noticed me in a couple scenes. I was there. Less beautiful, scripted with less erudition, less suavity. My wardrobe was selected for neutrality, my lines written for the simple advancement of plot. I made no bold declarations, no professions of love. I delivered the facts so my more prominent, more romantic counterparts could voice lines as if reciting poetry. The soft focus of their faces filled the whole screen for every smile and tear, while I stood, smallish, in the perpetual background of my existence.

They're all gone now, as the real names of the people who pretended to be them scroll up the screen, accompanied by a swelling string orchestra (there goes the name of the man who pretended to be me). The copyright halts in the center of the screen and the music fades and then everything is black. This is usually when you leave, if not before. But we are still here now, together.

What is my name? Military Officer #2. On my costume, on an embroidered patch, chest-high right, it says Pendleton. My rank insignia makes me a colonel. But in the script I am identified only as Military Officer #2. I am too young to be a colonel. I know this, and you, the observant viewer, must have noticed it. I have no obvious subordinates, partake of no battles, lack even a gun. But I am Military Officer #2. I will tell you my story.

There is an explosion, shown from many different angles so you can appreciate the pyrotechnics. I am with a group of people like me. Soldiers and Lab Techs and Townspeople. Lab Tech #1 and Military Officer #1 are shown in close-up, tears of admiration in their eyes (tears that net them considerably more pay than the rest of us). Then you are looking down from a helicopter. The view pulls farther out and the fire is a small yellow speck on the landscape. An ocean creeps into view. It is supposedly the Pacific but we filmed on the coast of Maine. The camera pans up until the screen is filled with sky. Fade to black. Credits.

We are on a vista, those of us still alive, overlooking the burning facility. This is the sort of location that you only ever see in movies. You've never experienced a vista from which you can watch important action. Important action happens where it will, with little regard for scenery.

The explosion wasn't that impressive to us. It won't realize its onscreen glory until the digital effects people get their hands on it. They will expand the ball of fire. They will add a shower of debris and plumes of smoke. Maybe even a mushroom cloud. Was there a mushroom cloud? I have no way of knowing until I sit beside you, watching myself watch the thing that wasn't actually there for me to watch.

One by one we walk away, leaving Lab Tech #1 and Military Officer #1 behind. Their close-up has separated them from the rest of us. One day you will see them in a different movie and wonder where you've seen them before. You will wonder for days. You will wake up in the middle of the night and remember. *The vista*. There were other people with them, but you remember only these two.

Townsperson #3 walks with her head tilted back, looking up at the forest canopy. She has known this forest for as long as she can remember, as long as she doesn't remember too far back. This whole Californian coastline is her home. These trees, the likes of which do not grow in California, are hers, as are the species of birds unique to the East Coast, and other animals, and the color of the ocean.

Behind us, the facility continues to burn, making loud cracks, sounds that will be replaced in the final version of the film with a steady roar. The cracking fades as we move farther away. You'd think we would be upset, but we knew all along the fate of the facility. It was there in the script. We knew the flames before we saw them.

I've forgotten how long the walk back to town is because we've been cutting from one place to another with impossible immediacy for the last two hours. Beads of sweat burst through the layer of makeup on our faces. Solider #5 wipes his forehead with his sleeve and smears flesh tone across the camouflage fabric. Two of the older Townspeople stop and rest on a rock. We leave them behind. The scene on the vista was their last.

The trees thin out and the low buildings of the town become visible. Once white walls yellowed by time, small square windows full of yellow light. Towns like this, lethargic and homey, are perfect counterpoints for the action of a movie like ours. Through convention, when seen on screen, instead of providing the comfort they would in reality, these towns instead inspire agitation. You are conditioned to anticipate the shattering of the illusion of tranquility. Plus you've seen the previews. Before you ever sat in your seat in the darkened theater you had seen the final explosion, from at least two of its dozen angles, many times on TV. The last time you came to the movies, prior to the movie you had come to see, you were treated to three minutes of this town overrun with gunfights and car chases. You've seen beneath the surface. But it is a real town, not a set, and outside the realm of our movie it is, in fact, peaceful. With the main characters dead and burned up and resting comfortably in their trailers, there is nothing to upset the image of this town. It is what it looks like. You may abandon your previous apprehension. If this weakens the plot of the story I'm telling now, then so be it. I will lie about this town no longer.

The streets are empty except for those of us returning from the vista. The crew has already packed up all the equipment and rolled out in the trucks. The extras have gone back home. Most were from neighboring towns. They are left unmentioned in the credits. They sat next to you in the theater and waited for themselves to appear on screen, pointing out stray limbs in the tangle of crowd shots, claiming ownership of this hand or that elbow. You shushed one of them.

The actual townspeople, as opposed to our Townspeople, are all at home eating dinner by now. At first they were excited when the film crews arrived. They stood behind tapelines and watched as famous people said things to other famous people. But after weeks and weeks of disrupted lives, I know they will be glad to see us go.

I tell Solider #2 to get me a cup of coffee. It is the last time I will have this authority. I will remove the uniform and everyone will remember that I was never a solider, much less an officer. I sit on a bench in the town square. The square is a small grassy spot where they planted trees instead of built buildings. The grass around the base of the bench has grown taller than the top of my boots. Lab Tech #7 sits next to me, but we do not speak. We have no lines to say to each other. Soldier #2 never returns with my coffee.

Several Townspeople claim the gazebo in the middle of the square. They are talking and laughing and sharing stories like old friends. They have known each other for years, though we all met only a couple months ago, and they have just together experienced the kind of adventure that doesn't usually happen to Townspeople. The first round of laughter is over and they realize that they have no other history, nothing much before the vista. They get up, patting shoulders and shaking hands. They walk each in a different direction, as if they were the debris expelled in an explosion.

Lab Tech #7 rises from the bench and walks off, her white lab coat billowing ghostlike behind her. I want to say goodbye, but I am unsure of exactly how I should say it. I am unsure of who is saying it. My uniform feels suddenly uncomfortable.

There are only three of us left in the square. Soldier #3 and Angry Townsperson hold hands on the other side of the gazebo. I see them as black shapes against the sunset. The clouds are distant and flat and gray. The trees barely have any green left in them. It is a beautiful scene but maybe too obvious. It announces the end too loudly.

We all, the men at least, tried to woo Soldier #3 from the first day of filming. I did my charming best over the cold cuts on the catering table to impress her. But there was Angry Townsperson. You recognize him from a TV show. He was younger then, just a kid, but you remember the cut of his jaw and now he has the broad shoulders to match. When he doesn't shave at least twice a day, a thick growth of stubble covers his cheeks.

The sun is gone over the horizon. The shadows kick up like dust. I watch the couple leave the square, still holding hands, and for a moment I forget their names. Jen and Ryan? No, that's not right. She is just a Soldier. He is a Townsperson, albeit an Angry one. I am a Military Officer.

The lamps flicker on in the empty park. I look down at my chest to remember my name, but I can't read the patch in the low light. The streets are still empty. People don't wander the streets at night in small towns. Nightlife is a phenomenon of the big city. I used to have a life there, in the city, before boot camp, before casting. It is a place that I would never have walked alone.

I round the corner and the darkness is overcome by the glow of a movie theater marquee. In mixed black and red letters it says the name of our movie. I fish money from one of the many pockets of my uniform and I buy a ticket. Inside, a zit-faced boy takes my ticket and salutes me. It seems like I have not seen a zit in forever. I salute back. It is an unfamiliar gesture. I am the highest-ranking officer in the movie, and have been, until now, on the receiving end of all salutes. My fingertips touch my eyebrow and it is unclear which part of me is feeling the other.

The theater is dark. I follow the little lights in the floor and ascend the steps. I move into the row. I sit down next to you. Now you are part of the story. You were the audience, now you are The Audience. There is no one else in the theater. It is too dark to see your face. We'll call you #1. Audience Member #1. Don't say anything until you're supposed to. And never, ever look at the camera.

Single

I'm in the park reading. I was reading in my apartment, but I came down to the park so a woman would notice me reading. Finding interest in the book or in the reader, she would talk to me. She would crave my touch and I, craving something to touch, would be interested in her. I would set the book aside, and when we left for coffee and the eventual copulation I would forget the book. I would not forget it. I would leave it for the next sad, lonely man in need of something to touch.

The park bench is hard and uncomfortable. It is covered with pigeon shit. I'm sitting on the only stretch of bench equal to or greater than the width of my ass not covered with pigeon shit. A woman jogs by. She is a jock and doesn't seem interested in men who read. Maybe I should take up a sport. Badminton, perhaps. I am skinny, but not from exercising. Sometimes I sit on the park bench all day and forget to eat. I get up and run a lap around the bench. I sit, exhausted.

My favorite part of reading is the period. It is the simplest mark possible. I would read a whole book of them. An endless ellipsis. Or a single period, so large it extends beyond the edges of the page.

Three homeless men huddle on another park bench farther down the walkway. They are arguing with each other, but pause in their disagreement as the jogging woman approaches. They ask her for money. She smiles at them, but does not stop jogging. The homeless men resume their argument.

A new jogging woman approaches. She is not a jock. Her flesh is loose and whatever tone her muscles have is hidden beneath it. I set my book down, and as she passes I ask her for money. She pretends not to notice me, but there is no way she didn't hear the question. She jogs more quickly.

One of the homeless men walks over. He is wearing an olive drab army jacket from the Vietnam era covered with unidentifiable stains. His wiry beard projects from his face like an alert porcupine. His gray eyes rest deep in leathery, lined skin. He leans close to me. He smells like a public restroom. Gesturing to the other homeless men, he tells me to stop stealing their shtick. I apologize and continue reading.

A bear approaches. The bear is on a leash, held at the other end by a young woman. It is not a bear, but a large dog. It is not bear-like at all except for its unusual size. The dog's body is sleek and its presence noble. It is more like a horse than a bear.

I tell the woman I like her bear. She chuckles. The woman's shorts are cut high so that the bottom of her ass hangs out just enough to suggest the whole thing. She wears a tank top, and I can see the strap of her bra, which is pink. She asks me what I'm reading. *A book*, I say, because I can't remember the title. I have been paying attention only enough to know to turn the pages. I recall that the book contains many dates. *A history book*, I amend. She asks if I like history. *More than the present*. She chuckles again. This is what is called rapport.

She sits on the bench, not seeming to care about the pigeon shit everywhere. Her bear-dog sits in front of her. The three of us sit. The three homeless men, also sitting, watch us sit. They stop arguing to watch us. We are more interesting than their argument.

She asks me what I do. *Mostly sit on this bench*, I say.

I ask her what she does.

She answers. *I wander with my dog from park to park in search of something that was lost. This is not necessarily something that I lost, but it has been left to me to search for it. What was lost is fundamental, something stitched into the fabric of the universe, black silk patterned with silver vines and shells and feathers and skulls. It is a sphere that starts from nothing, grows until it is several meters across, then shrinks back to nothing. To glimpse it, I think, would answer many questions.*

She looks at me and I am uncomfortable. She is looking at me like I am the thing she is looking for. Her top lip is thin, but her bottom lip is swollen into a perpetual pout, one that is playful, taunting. Her bear-dog lies down and curls into itself. It forms a large hairy mound on the sidewalk. It makes a sound like a growl or a yawn. The sound is a little bit of both.

The woman's eyes are deep and black. Silver light glints off their surface in a pattern like branches or bones. She blinks slowly. Her eyes do not leave mine. The irises grow. They swallow me. The park around me recedes. The bench loses its substance. I float above the sidewalk. The sidewalk disintegrates in a puff like baby powder. The gray powder fills the whole sky. The ground crumbles to nothing and I'm surrounded by grayness. I see the three homeless men fall away through the void until as specks they disappear. I inhale but there is no air.

A black sphere grows before me.

Cockpuncher

John Cockpuncher thrust out his hand toward me. I didn't recognize the gesture and stared blankly at his extended arm. He laughed, good-naturedly, and explained the mechanics of the handshake. I smiled back, took his hand and shook it too hard, too fast. He laughed again and ushered me through the front door into his house.

The entryway was small and crowded with the rest of the Cockpunchers, lined up against the back wall like the family portrait that hung above their heads. The mother, Matilda, who insisted I call her Matty, stood between her son and daughter, Warren and Natalie. The three of them smiled at me. Matty came over and hugged me tightly. She smelled of baby powder and baked goods. Warren shook my hand, and I performed the gesture better on this, my second attempt. His grip was strong. He was the older child, a senior in high school, and already possessed an air of worldliness.

Natalie greeted me without moving forward. A smile flashed across her lips, puffy and pink. She blushed and lowered her gray-blue eyes. I followed her gaze to the floor, which was waxed to perfection, reflecting back over the wood grain an image of everything that rested on top.

Warren grabbed my suitcase, and I followed him into

a hallway hung with photographs of younger versions of the children. In every picture they smiled. In every picture the sun was shining.

My room was small but impeccably clean, like it had never known dust. The window looked out onto the backyard where thick green grass and a well-manicured garden stretched to a whitewashed fence at the edge of the property. Warren put down my suitcase. I sat on the edge of the bed and sank into the padding. I commented on its softness, and Warren apologized, saying that because it was the guest room the mattress wasn't as nice as the others in the house. He offered me the use of his own room, but I said it was no problem and that I'd not meant to complain. He smiled again, straight white teeth framed in a perfect crescent.

"I'll leave you to get settled," he said. "Dinner's at six. Hope you like meatloaf."

"Of course." I didn't know what meatloaf was.

⁘ ⁘ ⁘

I closed the door and unpacked my suitcase. I found the chest-of-drawers empty and I placed my boxers and socks inside. The closet was bare but for two dozen wooden hangers. I had only T-shirts and jeans with me, so I hung them. I took out my toilet kit. I didn't know where the bathroom was, so I put the kit on the end of the bed. Lastly, I removed The Jar and placed it on the nightstand. I shoved the now-empty suitcase into the bottom of the closet and slid the door shut.

The Jar caught the light coming in the window. I pushed it to the center of the nightstand on which there was also a framed photograph of the Cockpunchers. From my perspective it looked like they were trapped inside the glass. I thought about opening The Jar, letting them out. I wiped a smudge off The Jar with the bottom of my T-shirt, stood, and took my toilet kit to find the bathroom.

❖ ❖ ❖

The tile was pure white, reflecting back the entire spectrum with a pearly sheen. It covered the floor and came halfway up the wall. The rest of the wall was painted a flat, pale blue. In the center of the floor rested a bathmat, the same color as the paint, with thick pile that swallowed up my feet.

In the mirror I found my hair matted and tangled after many days of travel. I ran my fingers through it and it fell mostly into place. It felt in need of washing.

Natalie's blond head poked around the doorframe. Her eyes caught mine in the mirror. She blushed instantly. I turned and smiled at her. She looked down at the perfectly white floor.

"So you're from another country?" she asked. Her voice was small, delicate.

"Yep."

"And now you're here."

"Standing right in front of you."

She pointed at the mirror. "And I'm standing right behind you."

"Trapped in the glass."

"Is that why you're here? To trap us?"

"You've got it backwards."

"I saw your jar."

"Yeah, about that . . ."

She stepped fully into the doorway and faced me. "What's in it?"

I smiled at her, turned, and put my toothbrush into the medicine cabinet. In the mirror I watched her walk away.

⁂ ⁂ ⁂

The meatloaf tasted delicious, like a hamburger with the ketchup cooked inside. I had a second helping and half of a third before the Cockpunchers told me to save room for dessert.

During the meal John asked about everyone's day. While the kids were at school Matty had gone to a friend's house to do some knitting. Warren had aced a test in Calculus and then led a productive football practice as the team's quarterback. When Natalie was asked, she looked down at the white lace tablecloth.

"The same as usual," she said.

John turned to me. "And what about your day?'

"I caught a plane to Azerbaijan, where I had an hour layover. From there I flew to Osaka where I caught a plane to Minsk. My connection in Minsk was delayed, so I took a nap in the terminal. I woke up just in time to board. We were stuck on the runway for another hour because of fog, but finally we took off and landed in Jakarta a few hours later. Then I flew to Burbank, on to Green Bay, south to Austin, to New Orleans, and then finally I got here."

Matty chuckled. "What a long day."

Dessert was pie baked with apples, sprinkled with powdered sugar across the top. As John cut each slice, steam rose from the still-hot innards and carried the warm, inviting scent across the room. I ate one piece and asked for another. Warren warned that I would get fat if I kept eating so much. His warnings did not dissuade me.

Matty cleared the plates from the table. I offered to help,

but she refused to let me. So instead I sat in silence with the remaining Cockpunchers, looking over the floral centerpiece at each of them in turn. I grew tired as my body struggled to digest all the food I'd eaten.

Natalie looked up from the table and her eyes met mine for the first time since before dinner.

"What's your country like?" she asked.

"It's unremarkable, except there are yaks everywhere. I don't understand why, but we have an overabundance of yaks. You take the elevator up a skyscraper, get off on the twenty-seventh floor, and there is a yak waiting for you. How did the yak get up there? Did it use the elevator? Did it climb the stairs? No one is ever sure, but they accept it."

"And your family?" asked Warren.

"My parents died when I was young. My uncle raised me. He works with glass, making bottles and jars."

"He makes them by hand?" asked John.

"It is the only way to make them. Such a vessel must be crafted with care."

Natalie's eyes widened. "And what does he put in the jars?"

"Oh, you know . . ."

⁂ ⁂ ⁂

That night in the unfamiliar softness of the bed I slept fitfully. I dreamed of a yak inside The Jar on the table beside me. It spoke to me in Natalie's voice, asking questions about containers and the things contained within them. *What do you put in a sock drawer? What do you put in a closet? What do you put in a condom?*

I awoke with sweat on my face and an erection in my

boxers. I waited a minute for the turgidity to subside, then went to the bathroom and splashed cool water over my eyes. When I looked in the mirror, the yak was there behind me. *What do you put in Tupperware?*

"Leftover pie," I said to the reflection of the yak.

When I turned around, the yak was gone.

Back in the bedroom, there was no yak in The Jar, either.

I rolled onto my side in the bed, and I saw Natalie peeking in around the edge of the door. I felt a new stirring in my boxers.

"How did that yak get here?" she asked.

"No one is ever sure," I said. "It's best to just accept it."

⁂ ⁂ ⁂

The next day I followed Warren and Natalie to the bus stop. The air was cold and it stung my face. Warren had lent me a jacket. It was too large and the sleeves hung down past my hands.

The bus arrived. The door opened and Warren got on first. He sat with a friend in the second row. I followed Natalie to the back. The other students looked at me then looked away like they hadn't been looking in the first place. They all wore stocking caps. I moved more quickly to escape their gazes and bumped into Natalie. She had stopped by the last row. There was a yak in the seat to the left. She sat down on the right and I sat next to her. *What do you put in a school bus?* asked the yak.

I ignored it.

⁂ ⁂ ⁂

School was long and boring. One teacher droned on about the meaning of a book, the next about algebra, the next about mitochondria. The other students doodled in notebooks or stared out windows at the freedom that awaited them at the sound of the bell. Natalie looked down at her desk.

I followed her through the crowded hall. Lockers slammed on either side of us like cymbal crashes. The fluorescent light made me queasy.

The last class of the day was history, and the teacher took a special interest in me. He made me sit up front, and as soon as everyone else was seated he made me stand and introduce myself.

"Why don't you tell us about where you come from," he said.

"There's not much to tell. My country is far away from here. Seventy-two hours by plane. The land is mountainous and arid except for the rainy season when white clouds cover the whole sky. People speak one of seventy-two different dialects, though they all share a common word for glass. Glass is the primary export. You have probably encountered our glass before, in the windows of your churches or the moonroofs of your minivans."

"And jars," said Natalie from her seat in the back.

"And jars," I said, "and bottles and various glassware."

I sat down. The teacher thanked me and then began explaining the political history of my country. I was fascinated because I had never heard it before. The teacher told of kings and queens and princes and the plots and poisons that had killed them. He told us why the current democracy was much better, and he used the word *freedom* over and over.

⁂ ⁂ ⁂

When we got home the house was empty. Natalie pulled the dangling end of the chain around her neck from the confines of her shirt. A key hung from it. She unlocked the door and led us inside.

"Mom's off knitting," she said. "Dad's at work. Warren's at football practice."

Natalie locked the door. She walked across the room and lit the gas fireplace.

I moved toward the hallway to go to my room, but she stepped in front of me.

The house was not empty. There was a yak peering from the hallway. *What do you put in a cockpit?* asked the yak. *What do you put in a trunk?*

"What's in the jar?" asked Natalie.

"It looks empty," I said.

"But it's not."

She stepped toward me. She smelled of pure white flowers. The yak was gone.

⁂ ⁂ ⁂

That night I dreamt of a yak in The Jar. It moaned in Natalie's voice.

⁂ ⁂ ⁂

I awoke to the sound of the lawnmower. Outside the window Warren was cutting the grass while John and Matty tended the garden, though I saw no flaw with the present state of the yard. The sun was shining. There was no thermometer but I was sure it was 72 degrees.

I rolled out of bed and went to the bathroom. Still half-asleep I brushed my teeth. Natalie came in, but I didn't notice. She reached around me and slid her hand across my crotch. I jumped.

"Don't worry," she said. "They're all outside."

There was a yak in the bathtub. *What do you put in a hat? What do you put in a pocket*?

The yak jumped up and down in the bathtub. *What do you put in a mouth?*

Natalie reached back and closed the door. She turned me around by the shoulders. She sank to her knees.

⁂ ⁂ ⁂

I spent the rest of the morning in my bedroom, staring out the window. John and Warren finished the yardwork and Matty picked up her trowel and walked to the house. I heard them come in the door, move around inside. One by one they went to the bathroom and showered off the sweat and the dirt.

I rested my hand on top of The Jar. Through my fingertips I sensed a faint thrum. Something invisible was moving inside. It tapped at the lid.

"What's in the jar?" asked Natalie.

She had entered the room and stood behind me, looking over my shoulder. I saw her as a distorted reflection in the glass of The Jar. The thrumming grew stronger. It made a sound.

"It's trying to get out," she said. "What's in the jar?"

"It's knowledge, or so my uncle told me."

She walked around me and put her hand on top of mine.

"What is there to know?" She gestured out the window. "Grass isn't that green. No one aces calculus. Nobody knits anymore. There's no such thing as love."

I looked at her pale blue eyes without looking into them.

She kissed me on the cheek. "What we have is better."

"What we have is real?" I asked.

"Open the jar and find out."

A yak poked its head out from under the bed. *What do you put in a bottle? What do you put in a jar?*

⁘ ⁘ ⁘

We sank into the softness of the bed, and I cradled The Jar in my lap between us. The glass felt warm even though the air in the room was cool. Natalie took my hand and touched the tip of her tongue to my palm. She set my hand on top of The Jar. She grinned like she couldn't help it.

I twisted off the aluminum lid. It hissed and a large white flower bloomed from the space inside. The petals were wavy and delicate, their edges soft like down. It smelled of baby powder and baked goods. The flower finished growing and sat still for a moment. Then in a puff it turned to white mist and streamed out the bedroom door as if on a fierce wind. Natalie laughed out loud.

The sound of shattering glass returned from the hallway.

I ran out of the bedroom. Warren was on the floor, curled up in a ball. A broken picture frame rested beside him. I heard Matty crying from the living room. John was in the bathroom, staring wide-eyed into the mirror. He reached up and touched the reflection of his face with two fingers, like he didn't recognize himself.

He saw me in the mirror. His eyes watered.

To my reflection he said, "Cockpuncher really is a terrible name, isn't it?"

Natalie stepped into the hall, over the trembling form of her brother, and skipped to a stop in the living room where the white mist hung thick in the air.

She breathed in deeply.

The Tunnels They Dig

I am not floating. I am falling.

Below me is the sky. I am falling toward the sky. I will never reach it. I will never reach it alive. What once was me, long since starved of oxygen, will graze the atmosphere. My corpse will flare. It will vaporize. It will become gas. It will become part of the sky.

I am falling toward myself.

Very slowly.

I am surrounded by a thin shell of air that is held in place by this ridiculous suit. I am also surrounded by the sound of my breathing. My breath is the air made loud. Sometimes it fogs the glass of my faceplate. My breath is the air made visible. It only hangs there for a moment. The glass resists the fog. It is special glass made specifically for that purpose. And to keep out cold and radiation. I blow my breath against the faceplate to watch the air fade away.

I hit my head in the explosion.

I am not thinking clearly. I am aware of this, but unable to do anything about it. The very fact that I cannot think clearly prevents me from trying to clear my head.

I have spun so that I am facing down at Earth. I am facing the direction I am falling, like a skydiver. I spread out my arms and imagine the wind rushing past. My breathing provides the sound effect. Whoosh.

My spinning continues and now I face the spaceship. The windows glow orange. That would be the fire. Something sparked in a computer console. The smell of burning rubber filled the cabin. I pried off panels and opened compartments. I could not find the fire. It flared up from behind the attitude controls. By then it was too late.

The other astronaut was a scientist. She was studying worms and the tunnels they dig when weightless. When falling. The bulkhead behind her experiment exploded. The explosion threw me against the wall. I hit my head. A piece of metal shot out, spinning, and sliced through the scientist's neck. Her severed head bounced around the cabin. Her blood formed undulating orbs. I was a scientist studying the paths blood follows when weightless. I was charting the constellations in red.

I am an astronaut. I am an astronomer.

I abandoned ship and I am floating. I am falling.

In a small town in Indiana there is a pond where the ducks float on the water. They do not fall. They bob gently. The surface of the water ripples in the chill breeze. The clouds stream in from over Lake Michigan. On the shore of this pond there is a boy who will become an astronaut. He throws small pieces of bread into the water. The ducks paddle over and splash their bills against the surface. Sometimes a piece of bread goes unnoticed. It sucks up water from the lake. Slowly it sinks. Slowly it falls.

The boy was once bitten by a duck and he cried.

The tears gather in the corners of my eyes. When there are enough of them, they break free from my face and float in front of me. They float up to the faceplate. Some bounce off and some stick there. I spin to face Earth again. This time the view is obscured by my tears. They are like dots on the globe marking the cities toward which I am falling. The cities are all very sad. That is why they are marked by tears.

The spaceship comes back into view in time for me to see it explode. It is a bright, silent flash. The body of the ship cracks like a hatching egg, then pieces fly off in every direction. A number of large chunks hurtle toward me. I shield my face with my gloved hands, but the pieces sail past.

I am still breathing. My breath remains loud in my ears, gray on the faceplate. There is a gauge on the suit that tells me how much air I have left. I am not morbid enough to look. I do not need a countdown. A countdown is what brought me here in the first place. Three, two, one, fall.

I can see Earth again. Clouds cast shadows on the ocean. Something floats between me and the planet. I look at it. I look past the tears on the faceplate. It is one of the scientist's worms. It is what is left of the worm after a fire, two explosions, and explosive decompression. The little body is torn and mangled. It looks like an earthworm on a driveway, run over and dried out by the sun.

The worm moves. It is alive and wiggling. I am not a scientist so I do not know much about worms, but this does not seem right. It wiggles more.

I hold my breath. Something beeps inside my space suit.

The worm is floating toward open space. I do not know the escape velocity for a worm, but I know that this worm is free. It is free of falling. This impossible worm will wiggle into eternity. This worm alone will explore the cosmos and live the places that people dream.

I will not let it.
I will take the worm with me, or be taken with the worm.
I grasp at it with the thick fingers of my glove.
Worm in hand, I float away.

When as Children We Acted Memorably

The smell of chlorine brings back a memory of the strange cabin on the hill. Each time it is a different memory of a different cabin on a different hill. It is a memory of brick walls or stacked logs or Sheetrock. The windows were high and wide or triple-paned or thick and old and full of distortions. The view was of bald hills or forest or rivers ribboning into the distance. The only constant in the memory is the loose concept of a cabin and the smell of chlorine caught in the air.

Ricky's parents installed an above-ground pool the summer after we finished third grade. It never really got warm enough in our town for swimming, so it was the only pool any of us had ever seen, rising conspicuously from the rock-strewn backyard, forming a triangle with the doghouse and the yellow shed. It was made of straight panels, four feet wide, arranged in a jagged oval. I never bothered to count the sides then, to identify the shape more accurately. Dodecagon? Now, years later, it seems like an important piece of information, lost, except maybe in photographs stored in Ricky's parents' closet. If they're still alive. They were Asian, Ricky's family, and the only nonwhite people in our suburban neighborhood. His father did something for a corporation, earning enough to afford swimming pools and barbecue grills and trips to

Caribbean islands in the winter. I remember his father best, again, by a smell. The scent of cigars, over-pungent to the undeveloped sinuses of a child, followed Ricky's father like an olfactory shadow. In the evenings when Ricky's friends came over to swim, he greeted us with a terse hello. The cigar smell was complimented by that of whiskey on his breath. He was an intangible presence in the room, something I was aware of but couldn't wrap my hands around. A strong desire to hold something paired with the crippling inability to do so.

We settled into a routine, converging on the pool every day for the same set of games, the same races. After swimming, we would dry off with the gauze-like towels provided by Ricky's mother. She would have cookies waiting for us on the porch table, which sat in the one patch of sunlight that reached down between the trees and the roof of the house. The type of cookie changed each day, baked fresh, and the smell of baking is how I best remember Ricky's mother. She was the mother we all flocked to, wishing she was our own. After school we ran to Ricky's house and stayed there until dinnertime, often through it, a half-dozen children huddled around the too-small dining room table. Ricky's mother served us simple food, in nugget or sandwich form, on thin paper plates, and when we were done she whisked away the remnants before we could offer to help clear the table. She taught most of us our fractions. On our birthdays, Ricky's gifts, selected by his mother, were always exactly what we wanted. Later, after our mothers forbade us from going over to Ricky's house, I missed Ricky's mother more than anything. More than the pool, even more than Ricky himself.

That summer we learned to dive—unadvisedly—into the shallow pool. The first awkward bellyflops evolved into graceful needle punctures of the water's surface. We pulled ourselves up just before we reached the bottom, skimming it with our stomachs, bodies held in torpedo shape, letting momentum carry us forward and buoyancy lift us up. Most of us bruised elbows and knees, sometimes a head, but as we got better the injuries became less frequent. Ricky was the proud master of the pool. The undisputed champion of breath-holding competitions, the fastest swimmer, a tenacious Marco and an elusive Polo. He was the first to master diving and the most graceful. It was from him that the rest of us learned the subtleties of the art. With his encouragement we overcame our fear and entered head-first into the water. I remember him by his hair, a black mass, always messy, as if intentionally so. And his stance, proud but relaxed, as he stood shirtless by the pool, awaiting his turn to dive. Looking back, he was my best friend, though I suspect I am not the only one from our group who would claim the same thing. His absence is a palpable void in the universe. I know that somewhere, in some empty space, he *should* exist. I suppose he does exist, somewhere. What I feel, then, is my own ignorance as to the location of the space he inhabits.

Besides Ricky, the only other childhood friend I remember clearly is Lindsay. She was Ricky's opposite, awkward and flighty. She seemed to stumble with every step, tripping over flat sidewalks and stubbing her toes on anything that poked even an inch out of the ground. Her long blond hair, cobweb thin, was picked up by the lightest breeze and danced around her head like an electric halo. When she got out of the pool, her hair clung so close to her scalp that she looked almost bald. She spoke, when she spoke at all, in a high voice, high even for a young girl. She was the smart one, tasked with looking out for the rest of us. It was her small voice that warned us of oncoming traffic when we were about to dart into the street, or alerted us to the presence of overhead power lines when we swung sticks in mock sword fights. She was like a sister to me and Ricky, a figure of unassailable purity. Given the opportunity, in later years, we would have looked at her differently.

One day in the middle of summer, Lindsay mounted the deck and looked down at the pool. From behind her, those of us waiting our turn to dive urged her to hurry, but she just stood there, gazing into the rippling aquamarine, the lining of the pool lending its hue to the clear, filtered water.

"I see something," said Lindsay.

Before we could ask what she saw, she leapt high off the deck, inverted herself at the apex of her flight, and dove straight down into the water. The angle was too steep. There was no way she could pull up, no way she could avoid smashing her face into the bottom of the pool. She entered with barely a splash. We waited, breath held as if we were underwater. Lindsay did not resurface. Ricky was on the steps. I don't know if it was panic or instinct, or if something called him as it had called Lindsay. He bounded across the platform, and without hesitation, in a near-perfect imitation of Lindsay's dive, followed her into the water. I screamed his name, but he was already submerged. I scrambled up the steps and looked with terror at the bottom of the pool. There was nothing there. No Lindsay. No Ricky. I looked around the yard, trying to discern the nature of the trick, the means by which the two of them had perpetrated this magnificent illusion. But they were nowhere. The others, standing on the porch, mouths agape, looked at me. I shook my head.

Something seemed to move at the bottom of the pool, like seaweed waving in ocean currents, directly below where my two friends had disappeared. Before I could think anything, unable to think at all, I found myself making the same vertical dive into the water, aimed directly at the kelp-like something below. I opened my eyes wide and tried to scream but produced only bubbles. The floor of the pool rushed up. I swallowed a gulp of the medicinal water. I hit the bottom. But it wasn't hard. I passed into it as through a thick gel and floated there. The substance was warm and comforting, like the embrace of Ricky's mother, like the smell of fresh baked cookies. The longer I was inside it the more I relaxed, until, at the last moment, I felt like my mind left my body, and with it went all stresses and agitations. As a blank slate, I entered the cabin.

I dropped onto a mattress covered with a down comforter. When I tried to wipe the water out of my eyes, I realized that I was completely dry. Instead of my bathing suit, I was wearing old, unfashionable clothes, a sweater and pants I could imagine Ricky's father wearing when he was a child. I propped myself up on the bed. The room around me was the size of an average living room, and besides the bed, I saw a kitchen table, a sink, and a sofa. Ricky and Lindsay stood looking out a yellow-curtained window.

"Where are we?" I asked.

"I don't know," said Ricky, "but there's snow outside."

I half-hopped, half-stumbled off the bed and joined them at the window. The hill was bare of trees, and as far as could be seen undisturbed snow covered an undulating landscape, more hills like the one on which we found ourselves, but the others just a bit lower. I touched the window and felt the cold move from the glass to my fingertips. A circle of condensation formed where Ricky's mouth pressed near the pane. I looked at my clothes more closely. They were tailored for the environment, the sweater heavy and the pants thickly padded. The pattern on the middle of the sweater was of interlocking triangles, white on teal, the colors like the surface of the pool. Ricky and Lindsay were similarly dressed.

Ricky went to the door. He jiggled the knob back and forth, but it would not turn. He returned to the window and tried to push it open, but it was frozen shut. I joined him in attempting to raise it, but still it would not move. My hands felt numb where they had pushed against the glass, and I rubbed them together. Lindsay stood beside the bed, looking up at a point on the ceiling directly above it. A wisp of white energy hung there, like a tiny version of the Northern Lights. After watching it for many minutes, I realized it was the same as the kelp-like thing I had seen at the bottom of the pool. I had fallen into the room from that point. It was the portal.

That first cabin is the one I remember best. We spent much time there, inspecting each corner, the sparse furnishings, the grain of the wood-paneled wall. We tried to force open the door, each of the windows. None of them would budge, so we returned our attention to the interior. The circular rug in the center of the room, made from a coarse brown material, sprouting fuzz all over, was woven with a design of random green triangles. Leaning close, I first noticed, from the fabric, the smell of chlorine that would later define the whole experience. Once I had smelled it, I couldn't ignore it. It became overpowering, forcing itself up my nostrils, pounding inside my head. I grew dizzy. I saw that my friends were experiencing something similar, staggering under the attack of an unseen assailant.

"We need to leave," said Ricky.

"But how?" I asked.

"I'm not even sure how we got here," said Lindsay. "It was like a voice called out to me, and next thing I know I was diving into the pool."

Ricky gestured to the ceiling. "We'll go back the same way we came. The spot of light got us here, it must be able to take us home."

He climbed onto the bed, bounced slowly at first, then faster and higher, extending his arms straight out, spinning in tight circles as if dancing a dervish. Light descended like a liquid and surrounded him, suspending him in the air halfway between the bed and the ceiling. He spun there for a moment, wrapped in light, floating. Once per revolution he faced me, his expression slack, eyes closed, the countenance of sleep. His turning slowed, stopped. He opened his eyes and they were nothing but whites. Tilting back his head, he rose toward the ceiling. The light grew too bright to look at, filled the whole of the cabin with whiteness, washing out even the outlines of our bodies. I groped in blindness for Lindsay, to stabilize myself against the dizziness, to assuage my fear, but I found nothing. The floor beneath me lost substance. My body dissolved, turned to mist. I screamed with the mouth, throat, lungs I no longer had. All that came was silence, then gurgling. My head broke the surface of the pool. I gasped for air, though my chest was free from the burning sensation of held breath. The familiar sights of Ricky's backyard surrounded me—trees and slatted fence and the rough red-brown brick of the house. I was back in my swimsuit. Ricky and Lindsay stood with me in the water. Like any three points, we formed a triangle, but this one was special, the distance between us and the subtleties of the angles. I can't explain how, but I knew its specialness in the same way I knew to dive into the water and Ricky knew the way to return us home.

In the world outside the cabin, I had expected time to stand still. I had expected our friends to be waiting for us, waiting to hear the story of where we had been and what we had seen. I imagined them sitting on the deck, feet dangling in the water, faces to the sun. But the shadows had shifted to cover the yard and our friends were gone. There was no sign that they had ever been there. Usually we left a trail of towels and toys in our wake. But the surface of the back porch was empty, even swept free of fallen leaves.

"You're back," Ricky's mother spoke to us from the porch. "I was worried you would not return, as you spent much time in the cabin, long enough, surely, to feel its effects, the vertigo that overtakes you, that sends you spinning."

"Why couldn't we stay longer?" asked Ricky.

"It gets easier each time. It is a dangerous place, the cabin, but I know better than to forbid you to visit. You three form an interesting triangle. Maybe you can conquer that place. Maybe you can open the door."

She held out three towels toward us.

"Come," she said, "have some cookies. I just finished baking them."

Inside, fresh cigar smoke filled the house. I heard the sounds of a baseball game coming from the television in the living room. We passed Ricky's father and he looked at us, would not look away from us. I'm sure he kept staring in our direction even after we were out of sight, but he did not speak a word. In the kitchen, wrapped in the thin white towels, we ate cookies. My thoughts left the strange place we had visited and turned to the activities of the evening, the cartoons to be watched and video games to be played. I tried to speak of such things to Ricky and Lindsay but they remained silent, in their eyes the vacant look I had seen on Ricky's face as he hung above the bed in the cabin.

Our other friends, those who had watched us dive and disappear into the water, didn't come to Ricky's house again. When we saw them in the neighborhood, they would greet us like usual, sometimes join us in games, but something was strange. They never referred to the event, even when prompted, to the point that I am unsure if they remembered it at all. But they knew something. There was a reason why they wouldn't return to the pool, why their mothers shied away from us or took their children's hands if we approached. Sometimes when they talked I could hardly understand them. Ricky knew it, too. He distanced himself from everyone but me and Lindsay. I didn't mind, because I could lay more exclusive claim to the boy I considered my best friend. I could finally feel like the title went both ways, at least for a while. The power of our secret brought us together. I loved being in possession of the secret more than I cared for the secret itself. I loved our triangle more than the cabin.

On the day after our first visit to the cabin, we had returned to Ricky's backyard. We crept to the edge of the pool and looked down for the glowing spot on the bottom. It was there, in the same place, distorted by the rippling water, which was agitated by a gentle but ceaseless wind. This time I did not feel the compulsion to dive. That first time, I had felt beckoned, like I was being asked an important question that could only be answered through action, and so I had entered the pool not out of decision, but out of instinct. Now I felt, at most, curious, though in the posture of my friends, the way they leaned just a little bit forward, I saw that they were drawn to the bottom as strongly as before, and I knew that I would follow them. Eventually it became habitual—the more we visited the cabin the more we felt we had to visit, until it came to seem essential, at least for the other two.

Ricky dove into the water first, as he would each time we returned. As he neared the bottom, white light, flowing like milk in the water, surrounded him, faded, and he was no longer there. I let Lindsay go next. I watched as she, too, disappeared, and I stood there for a while in the steady breeze over the empty pool. My body trembled. It was not that I felt afraid, exactly. But I was already beginning to feel out of place, my point of the triangle obtuse to the acuteness of my friends. I felt necessary for the shape, as Ricky's mother had described it, but standing there alone, a point, without length or width, I doubted the necessity *of* the shape. They were already there, Ricky and Lindsay, and I was not, and sadly, it seemed not to matter. But my doubt was overpowered by the pending adventure and the desire to be with my friends, so I dove to the bottom of the pool, into the light, through the gelatinous something between the pool and the cabin, and I fell softly onto the bed in the corner.

The dimensions were roughly the same, but this cabin was constructed and furnished differently from the first. The walls were papered in a tacky flower pattern, the pinks too bright and the green of the leaves flat, lifeless. Against the far wall was a kitchenette with a small stove and refrigerator, microwave and toaster, a row of cabinets a few feet above the counter. A sofa, upholstered in fabric that looked to be selected specifically to clash with the wallpaper, occupied the center of the room, and it faced toward an old television set like the one on which Ricky's father watched sports, where the roar of the crowd came out robotically from built-in speakers. A rabbit-eared antenna sat on the TV, prongs angled in such a way that if they were connected across the top they would form a familiar triangle. Ricky and Lindsay were sitting on the couch watching a black and white movie. The actress on screen spoke with over-careful diction.

I went to the front door, thick and old and wooden, and tried to turn the knob, but it didn't even wiggle. Through the windows I saw tree trunks, almost atop the cabin, and looking up I could just catch a glimpse of the green forest canopy as it faded to shadow very nearby, the thick woods blocking the sun and making the afternoon feel like dusk. I went through the cabinets and found all sorts of food, some canned, some fresh. All of it looked newly bought. The same was true of the refrigerator. I took three apples and joined my friends on the couch and watched the incomprehensible middle of the movie with the strange-talking starlet. We finished our apples. Ricky stood.

"We should probably leave," he said, "before the dizziness starts up again."

Lindsay nodded. "I already feel like I'm about to tip over."

Ricky climbed onto the bed. He bounced, then floated, then disappeared in light. The light spread through the whole room. I watched the ugly walls as they were bleached into nonexistence, and I was warmed inside by the thought of homecoming. We were again in the pool, again formed our triangle. I tried to note the specific angles, to be able later to sketch the triangle on paper, but the exact shape eluded me.

On the deck, Ricky and Lindsay were overtaken by shivering as the wind, stronger now than before we left, licked across the wetness of their skin and carried away warmth with the evaporating water. I did not feel cold, however. I was aware of the wind, but to me it delivered fresh, familiar air. The whole time I had been in the cabin I had felt short of breath. Now, back home, I could again breathe normally. So the cold did not bother me and the faint prickling on my skin was like waking up.

Ricky's mother gazed out at us from the kitchen window. I thought she looked sad, but I couldn't tell because her face was dark behind the glass, which reflected back, over her, a faint image of the slatted fence. She saw me looking and moved away from the window. Moments later she came onto the porch with cookies that steamed in the cold air. I bit into a cookie as Ricky and Lindsay toweled off. The taste was of warmth more than flavor. As I chewed my first mouthful, Ricky's mother hugged me, quickly, as if she didn't want the action to be seen, and then went back inside. It was the last batch of cookies she baked for us. Ricky and Lindsay never seemed to notice their absence. But the cookies were all I could think of. How I hungered for them, more and more, each time they didn't appear.

We developed a routine for the rest of that summer. The three of us would gather at Ricky's house after lunch, already in our swimsuits. I didn't see Ricky's mother anymore as we passed through the house and out the back door to the pool. Sometimes I saw her in the kitchen window. Each time her figure looked darker, until it was nothing but a silhouette, and toward the end she disappeared completely.

Ricky would lead us into the water. Then Lindsay. By the time I arrived, the two of them were already engaged in whatever activity that particular version of the cabin had to offer. Sometimes we just stared out the window, amazed by the many landscapes the world had to offer. Sometimes we watched TV. The programs were different each time, always old, films and sitcoms representing, in black and white, a reality I could not recognize. I wonder now what my childhood reality would have looked like to a viewer in the distant future. Once we found the cabin furnished only with a ping-pong table. We spent the whole day there, returning to the pool long after evening had set in. Once, on a round table in the middle of the room, we found three pairs of binoculars, placed carefully as the corners of a triangle, and out the windows, alighting in a sparse forest, flocks of birds of every imaginable species. Once we found the floor covered with the scattered pieces of a massive jigsaw puzzle. We spent the afternoon assembling the edges, but when we returned the next day, both the puzzle and our progress were gone.

It was the last week of summer vacation. My afternoon visits to the pool were replaced by shopping trips with my mother to buy school supplies. She walked far ahead of me through the store, slinging items into her basket without asking me if I needed them. Pulling a staple remover from the shelf, she pressed it shut several times, the device like a biting mouth, before she placed it atop the pile in her basket. I followed her into another aisle, this one completely filled with pens, hung tightly-spaced on the pegboard, endless variations on color and ink and tip. I didn't see my mother stop in front of me and bumped into her. She was smiling at Ricky's father, Ricky beside him. Ricky hunched his shoulders and shifted his eyes away, and looked, just this once, small and meek. I tried to smile at him, but I couldn't. I didn't recognize in the boy before me the elements that made up my friend. I might not have recognized him at all if not for the scent of his father's cigars filling up the aisle.

My mother greeted Ricky's father warmly. She seemed not to notice Ricky. I realized for the first time that she didn't know Ricky as well as Ricky's mother knew me. Maybe all my mother knew of him was this timid boy before her now, his eyes downcast, hair unusually neat and parted. She asked Ricky's father how his wife was doing.

"She is as expected. I can feel her diminishing, as if she is falling away to a distant source of gravity that stretches her thinner and thinner."

"I understand," said my mother. "I know she didn't volunteer for such a thing, but it's admirable the way she bears it. I wish her well, and if I don't see her again, please let her know that I'll think of her, for instance, when I look in a mirror or lift a somewhat heavy object."

Ricky's father shook his head in an exaggerated motion. "It is not you who needs to express gratitude. Goodbye."

He moved out of the aisle. Ricky lingered for a moment, but he would not raise his eyes to mine. Eventually, he too walked away, and I caught my mother scowling after him with a look of disgust on her face, like a slap, that in later years would be directed at me. I followed her through the rest of the store as she bought school supplies as if for herself.

On the last Friday of summer vacation, I found myself free. I met Ricky in his backyard. We dangled our feet in the pool, and I recalled for a moment the simple pleasure of swimming, which we had forgotten, distracted by our trips to the cabin, so I slid into the water and swam laps until Lindsay arrived. She stood by the edge of the pool and looked around, slowly, pausing sometimes on the landmarks of the backyard—the large stone by the fence, the yellow tool shed, the doghouse that had housed no dogs of which I knew. I swam to the platform and splashed her with water. She laughed, and kicked a retaliatory splash at my face. I shielded my eyes, so I did not see Ricky cannonball into the pool, soaking Lindsay completely and sending a wave over the top of my head.

I was the last, as usual, to the cabin. In the room, other than the bed, there were three chairs, and nothing else, arranged in the shape of a familiar triangle. The walls were bare Sheetrock, painted white. No curtains hung over the windows, only cheap venetian blinds, retracted all the way to the top. The floor was tiled in one-foot-wide black squares with no gaps between, like in the halls of our school. I slid off the bed and looked out the window. Grassy hills spread away from the cabin, their edges crisp against the clear sky. Ricky and Lindsay already occupied two of the chairs. I took the third.

We talked. For many hours, we talked of everything we knew. We expelled the whole limited knowledge of our young existences. A story from one of us led seamlessly into a story from another. I felt a pleasant tightness in my chest, a euphoric relaxation of my limbs, warmth all over, blanketed in the company of these, my friends. Toward the end of our conversation, we recounted the discovery of the light in the pool, and we took turns recalling our many visits to the cabin. It was Ricky's turn.

"We arrived," he said, "and found three chairs in the center of a white room with a black floor. The chairs were arranged in a familiar triangle. We sat and talked for many hours, then we opened the door and left."

The door, set in a white frame, was a featureless black rectangle with a brass doorknob glinting suspiciously halfway up its surface. We rose from the chairs as one and moved to the door, maintaining the shape of our triangle as we went. Ricky gripped the knob, turned. The smell of grass rushed through the open door, chasing away the familiar chlorine stench. I blinked in the sudden sunlight. Ricky stepped outside as if into his own backyard, then Lindsay, but I remained motionless, unable to will my feet to follow. Reaching across the threshold, I grabbed Ricky by the shoulder, but he pulled away from me. My hand slid down his arm to his hand, which I gripped as if to shake. He looked back, not at me, but at our joined hands, and I could not recognize in the boy before me the one I called my friend. I released him. As Ricky walked from the cabin, the space between us, ever growing, felt more real, more solid, than the air it was made from, the distance farther than the paces counted from there to here. The room flashed white behind me. When I looked, only one of the chairs remained.

I slid the chair over and sat in the open doorway and watched Ricky and Lindsay run off over the smooth green hills. They ran with limitless energy, surging up each slope, disappearing over each crest, only to emerge again on the face of a hill even more distant. Toward the horizon the hills grew gray, the farthest completely desaturated and indistinguishable from the sky. I thought to follow, to sprint after, calling out for my friends to wait, but instead I sat, silent. I don't know why I didn't follow. I missed them immediately, felt deflated, empty, but I missed them like they had died, a hopeless sort of emptiness that no action could relieve. The people they had been, the children who were my friends, were gone, irrevocably, and those two I watched running away from me were other people altogether, strangers. They crested the farthest hill, stick figures against a backdrop of clouds, and I heard, even from this distance, their laughing, joyous, primal, as they slid, finally, from view.

I closed the door and twisted the lock. They would not be back, I was sure of that. I sealed the cabin, pulled the blinds, feeling the whole time very much like I was burying myself. In the dark, the glowing spot on the ceiling looked more solid, less wisp-like, and it called to me, stronger than it ever had. I realized my trips to the cabin weren't for the cabin itself, or for the sense of adventure, but for the solidity of friendship, and now that my friends were gone I was called to a home where I might, eventually, make new friends to replace those I had lost.

I jumped on the bed, mimicking Ricky's movements as best I could, bouncing, higher and higher, impossibly high, lifted by an unknown force. As I spun, it felt like the cabin revolved around me, like I was suddenly the center of the universe. The spot on the ceiling spread, light descended and enveloped me, a warm feeling like a towel that has been resting in sunlight. Whiteness filled the room, and as it faded I felt the water of the pool wash around me, the scent of chlorine overpowering. I climbed out of the water, but found no towel waiting for me. I stood there for a long time, letting the sun dry me, in a wind that carried unfamiliar smells from distant places.

It was quiet in Ricky's house, absent the familiar sound of the television. I called out to Ricky's mother. I needed to tell her Ricky was gone. I needed to tell her everything. I smelled cigars and turned to find, looming over me, the whole mass of Ricky's father. He looked at me like he didn't know me, like he had never before seen a child. He knelt so that his eyes were at the level of mine, but I cannot recall his face, and remember instead darkness, a black cloud of cigar smoke in the shape of a man. He gripped me, painfully, by the shoulders, as if to affirm the solidity of his form.

"You're back," said Ricky's father. "You had an infinite world before you, and yet you return."

I saw Ricky's mother behind him. She was in a wheelchair, withered, skinny to the bone, gray-haired where once it had been black. Her hands, nimble in the preparation of meals and the baking of cookies, were now gnarled, fingers hooked toward palms, knuckles swollen. The skin of her face sagged, and the only recognizable thing about her, amidst the loose flesh, was her eyes, which looked at me, I now realized, with gratitude. I broke myself free from the grasp of Ricky's father and embraced her. She hugged me back, but weakly—so weakly I started to cry for everything that had ever been lost.

I said to Ricky's mother, "They ran from the door, across the hills, until they disappeared in the distance. They didn't even say goodbye."

"Nor should you," said Ricky's father. "It was not supposed to happen this way. Look at her," he thrust a finger toward Ricky's mother. "She is frail as an autumn leaf. You came back, and so this little bit remains. Now she will stay withered and the rest of us will age and the promise of eternity grows more distant with each step you take in this world. Leave now, and never let me see you again."

I was too young to understand it, and even now it is unclear what was at stake. Ricky's mother knew she had to let us go but loved us too much to do so. By coming back, I let her have both: the holding on and the release. I worry sometimes, though, that maybe it was neither.

Ricky's mother reached after me as I opened the front door and stepped outside. Before I ran from the door, down the street, parallel to the line of similar houses, I spoke to her for the last time.

"I bounced on the bed and spun in the air and vanished in the light."

Use Your Spoon

"I sense an awful strength within me."
—Daniil Kharms

1

When I was seven I did not perform my first miracle.

On the tips of bare toes, arm stretched so far it hurt, I placed the final red brick. This was the top of my tower. I had more Legos, but I could only reach so high. I stepped back to see what I had created.

It should have been a moment of triumph. But looking at the little red block at the top of my tower I wanted it taller. It wasn't even a want. I felt no desire. I simply sensed that I had, within me, the ability to make it taller.

Shadows spread across my bedroom. The lamps didn't dim, the sun didn't set, but it was like something around me pushed away the light. The windows were closed, but gusts of wind lifted papers off my desk. Crayon drawings and pages marked with my childish scrawl flapped around me. I heard popping and realized the noise came from my hands. Blue sparks leapt from my fingertips to the Lego tower, spiraling around it like climbing vines.

With the sparks from my fingers came the knowledge of my abilities. With a thought I could do anything, cause anything, create anything. I could reach any height. In my mind I saw a Lego tower to rival the architecture of Rome.

But what did it mean? I'd read Spiderman comics. Great power and great responsibility and all that. The word *responsibility* was synonymous with cleaning my room and feeding the dog.

The sparks faded, the wind died down, and the light returned to normal. I closed my fist and punched through the Lego tower. Bricks scattered across the floor. I dragged my bare foot through them. Their corners poked at my skin.

⁂ ⁂ ⁂

At the breakfast table the next morning I dumped milk over my Cheerios, spilling as much on the table as into the bowl. My mother didn't seem to notice.

The sun shone in the window over the kitchen sink, giving everything a lemon glow. The cheap dinette set. The chairs with chrome legs. The bowl, the Cheerios within. I pulled a few out with my fingers.

"Use your spoon," said my mother.

I ate the Cheerios.

"I'm a miracle worker," I told her.

"I always knew you were special."

"Thanks."

"What miracles can you perform?"

"Anything."

My mother got up from the table and took her plate to the sink. "Why don't you get your father to pay child support, then?"

"That's not really how it works."

I reached in again with my fingers and grabbed more

Cheerios.

Without turning around, my mother said, “Use your spoon.”

2

A dead frog sprawled in the pan in front of me. Its skin was milky brown and spongy to the touch. My lab partner, Natalie, pinched her nose at the smell of the formaldehyde. There were tears in her eyes.

“Are you sad?” I asked.

“Sad and disgusted,” she said.

The teacher stood at the glossy whiteboard, sketching a crude frog shape in blue marker. For the organs he used red. The finished product looked more like a map of an obscure island than an amphibian. He talked, but I didn’t listen.

“I’ve always kind of liked frogs,” said Natalie.

I poked our dead frog with the metal probe, as if trying to wake it from a nap. I wanted its eyes to snap open. I wanted its tongue to flick out as it yawned away murky dreams. I wanted Natalie to remain innocent in her like of frogs. What more did she need to know than their hopping?

I pointed my finger at the dead frog. Sparks arced into the rubbery body, sending spasms through the muscles. Natalie screamed and ran out of the room. Everyone was looking at me, but I had stopped when she screamed, so all my classmates saw was a confused boy and a dead frog. I shrugged.

The teacher followed Natalie into the hall. My classmates turned their attention elsewhere. I felt pained that I had frightened Natalie, when I only wanted to make her happy. A miracle, I learned, has unforeseen consequences. I flicked the frog with my finger.

It did not respond.

❖ ❖ ❖

I swallowed the last bite of my ham sandwich and slurped the last dribble of liquid from my juice box. The sides of the box caved as I kept sucking up the air inside. I released my mouth and the box puffed back into its original shape.

Natalie sat down beside me and set her tray on the table. Her lunch consisted of a rectangle of pizza and a carton of milk.

"I'm sorry about in biology," she said.

I shrugged. "Everybody screams."

"What were you doing?"

"I'm a miracle worker."

"You were bringing the frog back to life?"

"I guess so."

"What else can you do?"

"Anything."

Natalie picked up the pizza and took a bite. The cheese looked like the skin of the frog. She chewed thoughtfully then took another bite and chewed thoughtfully again. She put down the pizza.

"Can you make me feel love?" she asked.

I looked into her eyes but nothing happened.

"I guess not," she said.

Her eyes were very blue and beautiful.

3

I tried to pick out the music above the other sounds of the party. People danced in the next room. It was easier to see the beat in their movements than to hear it. Everyone was coupled up, boy-girl, boy-girl. They ground against each other. They held their beers high, red plastic cups suspended above the grind.

One of the frat boys came in and pumped the keg and thumbed the tap. Air sputtered out but nothing else.

"The keg's tapped out," yelled the frat boy.

Someone cut off the music. Those without drinks started moving toward the door. As the crowd thinned I saw Natalie standing in the far corner, sipping quickly from her drink without quite chugging.

I hadn't seen her since high school. I hadn't talked to her since long before that. Her hair was longer. She was in the middle of a group girls urging her to drink faster. Very few people remained in the room where they had been dancing.

I lifted the keg. It was surprisingly light. I wanted the party to continue. For that to happen, I needed more beer. I closed my eyes and felt the metal grow warm as sparks bounced around the empty interior. The room darkened.

It felt like beer was pouring directly into my brain, a layer of bubbles foaming just below my scalp. I leaned forward and couldn't stop the motion. My fingers slipped. The keg clanged against the floor.

I awoke to one of the frat boys shaking me, slapping me lightly on the cheek. I got up and rushed to the other room.

It was empty. Natalie was gone.

⁂ ⁂ ⁂

I sat at the counter in Mussolini's Pizza eating a slice. The crust was thin and greasy, sagging like wet paper. With each bite the fog in my head cleared a little.

The owner of the shop looked me up and down. He was a thin man with a fat face. A thick white mustache filled the space between his nose and lip and then some. He placed his hands on the counter and leaned toward me, shaking loose a dusting of flour from his skin.

"You look like hell," he said.

"I'm a miracle worker."

"You got sauce on your face." He gestured to his own cheek.

I looked down at my napkin, saturated with red-orange grease, and shrugged.

4

My apartment was small and overlooked the city. I could see all the beautiful architecture, but mostly I saw the ugly roofs. They were stained by water and washed out by the sun. Dirt and debris gathered in the corners. Once, in a nearby window, I saw a woman changing clothes who looked like Natalie. I called out her name, but the intervening space stopped the sound from reaching her. Or it was not Natalie.

Someone knocked on my door. Three quick knocks.

I cracked open the door. My landlady was outside. She filled up a large muumuu and the folds of her chin hung down over her chest. A smoldering cigarette dangled from between two of her beefy fingers.

"Rent," she said.

"Is it that time already?"

"You owe me for six months."

"Let me get that for you."

I closed the door and walked to the middle of the room. Where could I find three thousand dollars? I scavenged $4.53 from my pocket. I checked the cushions of the couch, but found only stale Cheerios.

I cracked the door.

“Six months?” I asked.

“In my hand right now or you’re evicted.”

“Just a moment.”

I closed the door.

Sparks jumped from my fingers. All the money I needed and more was only a snap away. I pointed at my palm and imagined the crisp green bills sitting there. I imagined the look on my landlady’s face as I handed her the money.

But no, a miracle is not for proving other people wrong.

I lowered my hand.

I pulled my suitcase from the hall closet and packed some T-shirts and some jeans and underwear and socks. I opened the door. My landlady was leaning against the opposite wall puffing on her cigarette.

I exited the building without saying a word.

⁂

My feet were propped up on the suitcase under a table at a fast-food restaurant. I bit into my burger and with my free hand I stacked ketchup packets on top of each other. I could only stack three or four before they tumbled over. A line of people stretched back from the counter and all the tables were full. In the back corner near the bathroom a baby was crying.

I finished the burger and started in on the fries. A young black man set his tray on the table and sat down in the seat opposite me. His bald head reflected the fluorescent lights. He had a double cheeseburger and a large fries and a drink I couldn’t identify through the cup. He gestured at my suitcase.

“Going somewhere?” he asked.

"Definitely somewhere."

He unwrapped his burger and the paper made crinkly noises.

"I'm a miracle worker," I said.

"What exactly does that mean?"

"Whatever, I guess."

He held his burger in front of me. "Can you heat this up? It's cold."

"You better take it back to the counter," I said.

The man shook his head and left the table.

I ate my fries and some of his and was gone before he returned.

5

Everything around me was brown.

I woke up in a cardboard box in an alley under an awning. The air was chill. My head rested on a wad of newspaper. My toes poked out of holes in my shoes. My stomach rumbled.

I crawled out of the box into the alleyway and stretched myself as tall as possible. In the next box over, Phil was waking up, too. He shuffled out and straightened his back and folded his knees under him and sat on his heels. Phil was old and his skin was milky brown, almost translucent.

"Mornin'," I said.

He grunted something that wasn't language.

It hit me without warning. My guts convulsed. I doubled over and fell to one knee. Phil came over and patted me on the back, then he walked off down the alleyway and out onto sunny Flotsam Street beyond.

My insides would not unclench, as if someone had stuck a fork in me and was twisting everything around like spaghetti.

I closed my eyes and breathed slowly until I could tolerate the pain.

I looked at my cardboard box.

I thought of a fine brick house with a kitchen and a refrigerator full of food. I thought of a dinette set with chrome legs. I thought of the cool touch of cutlery.

I looked at my cardboard box.

I pointed my finger. Sparks jumped to the cardboard. A gust of wind ripped through the alley, kicking up discarded newspaper and little bits of debris I couldn't identify. My brick house was just a thought away, but I saw Phil's box out of the corner of my eye. Then I thought of every box in the city. Every box in the world. And all my thoughts were packed away in boxes.

With a few last pops the sparks faded. I walked out of the alley clutching my stomach.

⁂ ⁂ ⁂

The line stretched out into the street. Men in holey sweatshirts and dirty jeans shuffled closer to the door one step at a time. Everywhere the faint scent of vinegar wafted through the cold air. I crossed the threshold into the warmth of the room.

Smiling volunteers ladled brown slop into Styrofoam bowls and handed one each to the disheveled men who walked by. Steam rose from the bowls. The scent of vinegar mixed with that of boiled meat.

Phil stood behind me in line. He mumbled gibberish to himself. The smiling volunteers filled my bowl. As they went to prepare Phil's, the ladle dinged against the bottom of the empty pot.

"I'm afraid that's all we've got," said one smiling volunteer.

I pointed at Phil.

"Give mine to him," I said.

"Are you sure?" asked the smiling volunteer. "You don't look so good."

"Don't worry. I'm a miracle worker."

"Oh, really? What can you do?"

"You know . . . whatever."

"How about a refill?" she said, gesturing to the empty pot.

"I don't think you understand."

I left my place in line and walked back outside. I walked all the way to the heart of downtown, through traffic and past business people in expensive clothes chatting on cell phones. I walked by storefronts filled with electronics and appliances and toys. I walked quickly, like I was trying to get away from something.

My insides hurt worse.

I stopped beside a green-glass skyscraper, the tallest building in the city. My stomach caved in on itself. I sank back against the glass, smearing my filth across it. I slid to the ground. People stopped to look at me. A smiling volunteer asked if I was alright.

I saw Natalie in the crowd. She didn't recognize me. Blue sparks flashed in front of my eyes, just a few of them, then nothing.

This Next Song

The man on the stage holds a banjo. He plays the banjo. He sings in a twangy voice but sometimes a Midwestern accent slips out. He sings love songs and sad songs about love. Black cloth is draped behind the stage so he sings sad songs in blackness.

This is my first date with Richard. I'm not gay, but I figured I'd give it a go. I mean, he asked so nicely. *Would you like to go hear some music?* He has a friendly voice. So we're sitting here listening to the banjoist. I sip black coffee. Richard sips some concoction it took the barista like fifteen minutes to make. The milk is fluffy. Who'd have thought of fluffy milk? It sticks in Richard's mustache until he licks it away.

Most of the people in the coffee shop are talking. They're having conversations about retirement plans and the medical maladies of their pets and other things that people talk about when they're not listening to the music.

A young woman sits by the front of the stage. She is skinny, almost unhealthily so, and has fine blond hair pulled back in a ponytail. She bobs her head to the music so that the ponytail bounces a beat behind. I am checking her out, which I feel bad about since Richard sprung the buck fifty for the coffee. Poor Richard. If only he knew what I'm coming to realize.

I am most definitely not gay. Mystery solved. Light the pipe and smoke it, Sherlock. Maybe we can just be friends, Watson.

The front door creaks open. It is silent, but the motion gives the visual impression of a creak without the accompanying sound. It opens as if the hinges are old and squeaky. A black man enters, hunched over, moving as if he too were old and squeaky. He jitters across the threshold and takes a seat by the back wall. He gives an impression of homelessness. He has a black bandanna on his head, tied so the corners dangle in front of his eyes. He is forever pushing the corners of the bandanna out of the way with a jerky movement of his hand.

The homeless man talks to himself. There is no one else near him to whom he might be talking. His hand jerks up and pushes the corners of the bandanna out of his eyes. What is he talking about, I wonder. He is very interested in the things he has to say. He nods, agreeing with all of his arguments.

I lean close to Richard and half-whisper.

"The selfless man is a myth," I say. "There's no such thing as a choice that doesn't benefit the chooser. Whether I eat the last cookie to satisfy my hunger or give it to you for the emotional gratification derived from generosity, either way I'm serving myself."

"Huh?" asks Richard.

I lean back, unable keep the frown from my face. I take the cookie from the plate between us. It is filled with chunks of toffee that stick to my teeth.

A final chord rings from the banjo, and the audience claps politely, fingers to palm, not the more enthusiastic palm to palm. Palm to palm is reserved for larger venues.

The banjoist strums the banjo, adjusting the capo on the neck. The chords he plays seem random, each plucked from a different song. It's like listening to the wandering of his thoughts.

"This next song," he says into the microphone, "is about love. It's rather sad."

He begins a slow, sad song about lost love. I don't consider the banjo a romantic instrument. It's not the tool of the serenade, but there is something of longing in its timbre. The short string on top pierces through the other sounds, like a cry in the night. It is animal and it is human. It is an animal eating a human. It is a human wishing not to be eaten. And that is longing.

Richard taps the back of my hand. I look at him, and he looks right back into my eyes, longingly. I yank my hand away and suddenly the slow, sad song is Richard's. He lowers his gaze to his compostable coffee cup and the fluffy milk within. Something like cinnamon is sprinkled on top.

I chug the remains of my coffee. Rising, I pat Richard on the shoulder and mouth *Thanks for the coffee,* but he doesn't look up to see it. I walk to the stage and take a seat next to the skinny blond woman. She smiles at me. I take a moment to think about lips, of which I find hers to be a pleasing example. Blood rushes into my ears and I can barely hear the song over the roar of my insides.

The banjoist sings:

When the sex dries up
And you realize
That you lack completely
Emotional or intellectual
Compatibility
Well, that puts a crimp in things

The old homeless man lurches forward. He bumps into my chair. He stumbles past me and stops, toes pressed against the stage. His hand jerks up and pushes the corners of the bandanna out of his eyes. Bringing his palms together he claps along to the beat. The tempo drags and the claps come only occasionally. Palm to palm.

For his part, the banjoist doesn't seem to notice the clapping, like he didn't notice the many people talking. Like he didn't notice the whoosh of the air conditioner or the grrrrzdddkkkk of the coffee grinder. There are so many things not to notice. The banjoist finishes the last verse of the slow, sad song, and begins the final refrain.

Lifting his face to the ceiling, the homeless man sings along. His voice spreads like thick paint, a high warbly tenor. The harmonies are unexpected, surprising, tense. They release into minor thirds and open fifths. They are tense again. The homeless man claps along, palm to palm.

The room has grown quiet. Every breath is held. Mouths hang half-open, unfinished words readable on the shapes of tongues. The only sound is the singing.

The two voices tangle together in a soaring double helix. A man in a flannel shirt stands and sways to the song, waving his arms above his head like at a revival. Asses slide to the edges of seats. I take the blond woman's hand in mine and squeeze it. She squeezes back. This is what they call a moment.

The banjoist and the homeless man hold the last note until their lungs give out, and still the banjo rings after them. Everyone exhales the breath they've held, but still no one claps. The man in flannel stands motionless, arms still above him, like he's diving upwards. Only the homeless man is still clapping to the beat of the already ended song. The banjoist looks down at the homeless man as if noticing him for the first time. He adjusts the strap on his banjo and crinkles his nose. He makes a shooing motion, fingers down, brushing away at the homeless man with the backs of his hands. The homeless man keeps clapping a slow beat, palm to palm. His hand jerks up and pushes the corners of the bandanna out of his eyes.

"This next song," says the banjoist, "is about love. It's rather sad."

He looks into the darting eyes of the homeless man and strums the banjo. The chords are disjunct and don't make any sense together.

He sings:

Go away, crazy man
Take your fidgets
Take your jitters
Take the subtle
But somehow overpow'ring
Scent of
Vinegar
The hell away from
Me

Go away, crazy man
Take your soupy eyes
Take your droopy cheeks
Take this subtle
But somehow overwhelming
Feeling
Of pity
The hell away from
Me

The homeless man fishes through his pockets and pulls out a metallic bubble gum wrapper. He smooths out the wrinkles, sliding the wrapper between his thumb and middle finger. It looks like a magic trick. I expect the wrapper to keep coming and coming, an endless silver ribbon. The homeless man drops the wrapper into the empty tip jar in front of the stage. For a moment his motions are deft, effortless.

His hand jerks up and pushes the corners of the bandanna out of his eyes.

Again the banjoist makes the shooing motion, at the same time thanking the homeless man for the tip.

Removing his banjo, gripping it by the neck, the banjoist smashes it across the top of the amp. There is a brief whine of feedback then silence. The audience claps, fingers to palm.

The old homeless man shuffles away from the stage. He pauses by Richard, who is still bent over what must by now be a cool cup of fancified coffee. The homeless man taps the table with two fingers. Richard looks up and sees the homeless man's extended hand. The skin is dry and callused, the texture of old asphalt. Richard reaches and takes hold. He rises, and hand in jittery hand the new couple walks out. I grin at Richard's broad back. Good for him.

The blond woman still holds my hand, the sweat of our palms intermingling. I reach up and stroke her cheek with the back of my finger. Again she smiles, stretching her lips free of wrinkles. I am reminded of sad songs about love, but I can't remember the lyrics.

The man on the stage holds a broken banjo.

One Has Hugs the Other Punches

My grandmother told me that when it rains and the sun is shining at the same time the Devil is beating his wife. What kind of woman marries the Devil, I asked her, but she wouldn't answer, smiling, eyes unfocused, into the distance of memory. She said:

The sound of rain on the stone roof and the creeping slice of light cast down on the floor. Tears, or was it blood bright against my cheek? The only sound a gasp that slipped from his lips as it happened. Like it surprised him. The ache in his knuckles. He never knew how to throw a punch, left his grip loose, and the pain just made him angrier. And he was an angry man to begin with. Red skin? Hardly. He was just always so mad. His blood welled up to the surface, all over. He'd kick at the stone walls and torture whatever happened to be around him.

Have I ever told you about his hair? Jet black. He was already an old man when I met him, but not a speck of gray. He spent a full hour every morning in front of the mirror, slicking his hair back so the widow's peak cut a perfect V down his scalp. If anything, his scalp was even redder than the rest of him. Heat rises, after all. I tried and I tried to get him to shave off that stupid little mustache, but he loved it. Waxed it every morning, sometimes traced the edges with eyeliner. The vanity! He never wore clothes. I can't blame him for that. That's the reason I got with him in the first place. It's like the body fat had all melted away in the heat of his anger. His muscles were ropy in action, round and smooth at rest. And, I know you don't want to hear this from your grandmother, but his member was magnificent. Of course it was large. The largest I've ever seen. But it was also the shape. When erect it shot straight out from his body and the artery on top would pulse with his heartbeat. And to touch it! It was steaming. When he removed it from . . . well, you know, the moisture would evaporate. You could watch it. A puff of steam. A little cloud made from our fluids. I called them our babies. Cloud babies. I'd watch them rise away and dissipate before long, but I always hoped that they kept rising, invisible, all the way up to . . . I wanted my babies to live somewhere more pleasant than Hell. Though let me tell you, for sure, that man shot blanks. With my second husband I had seven kids, your father included, and three miscarriages beyond that, and I never got down to it with your Grandpa, rest his soul, nearly as often as with that old Devil.

Obviously, the Devil loved pain, and what is sex if not the mutual pursuit of a pained release? After a day of dismembering sinners and boiling human flesh, he wanted nothing more than to feel a bit of that pain himself. And I gave it to him. Almost every night. Some he worked late. Those he'd come home and climb into bed straightaway without even dinner. But most nights we made love. I can't really use the word love with him. He was incapable of it. To him, it was weakness. Weakness was the one thing that scared him. It was always after the act, when he lay quivering, skin inflamed and sweaty, like red vinyl, that's when the shape of his face would shift. He'd scowl, and I knew what was coming. I mean, he always scowled, but this was a look reserved for me. I think he couldn't stand the thought of anyone seeing him in that moment. He wanted to *subjugate* me, if that's the right word. Or diminish me. I'd caused him pain. I'd seen him weakened. He wanted to return the favor. I'm not saying he thought it out like that, but I've had years of experience since, and your Grandpa was no saint either. The Devil would pick something about me that irritated him. My shoes left in the middle the floor. A steak that I'd undercooked—he liked them practically charred. Sometimes it would be something from days before. He'd focus on the littlest thing and project onto it this irrational rage. It built up in him so fast. It detonated. I'd try to calm him down, but it never worked. He'd swing, always at my face. That's where he looked when he bedded me. Never once at my body. Never more than he had to, anyway, to find where to put whatnot. So he knew me as my face. I had a great body as a young woman, but leave it to the Devil to focus on the eyes, like they are the gateway to the soul or something. Of course he knew better than to believe tripe like that, but what he knew and what he did rarely had anything to do with one another. He'd hit my face, hurt his hand every time, then plead with me to stay as I stormed out. I always took a couple laps around the fire pits, trying to find forgiveness inside myself, and I always did, and I went home and there he was at the kitchen table, and he wouldn't speak an apology, but *he* looked like the one who'd been beaten. Could I blame him for what he was, for being an evil outcast, shunned by his all-loving creator? He'd hug me and wouldn't say a word. I was so young, I thought the silence meant something. But no, it happened again and again, until one day when I walked away I just kept walking. Then I climbed. All the way up to the surface. My fingers were bloodied and my knees scraped. It had been years since I was last above ground and it was too bright for me to see and I only knew I was outside by the feel of rain on my skin.

Come on, Grandma, I said, there's no such thing as Hell.

I know I know, she said, but whenever I see rain like this, as if it fell from the sun itself, I can't help but think about the poor woman who's with him now. I can't help but hope that when she walks away she keeps walking. Rain like this is just *unnatural*.

The Loneliness of Large Bathrooms

With nothing else to do, in almost any situation, I count things.

Hotel lobby. Twelve people. Four couples. Remove eight from the equation. One man, three women. Two of the women, forty-plus. Remove three. One woman remains.

I smile at her from across the room. I stand and move to the bar. She follows, a few seconds behind. When she arrives I have already ordered two drinks. Vodka cranberry. It's a drink I've found most everyone likes well enough, especially women who follow strange men to bars. She sits on the barstool, shimmies into a comfortable position. The position does not actually look more comfortable, but it allows her to lean forward and rest her elbows on the bar. It is a position that thrusts out her chest. Perhaps this is a request for further thrusting?

There is a glossy black baby grand piano in a corner of the bar. A white-haired, white-mustachioed man plays familiar songs in unfamiliar arrangements. I have never heard "Take Five" orchestrated so lushly. Its carefree bounce is replaced by a forced, false emotion. We are told how to feel, and for the sake of convenience we allow ourselves to feel that way. Like a shot of alcohol, it is a shot to the system. Immediate effect is favored over the delicacy of the flavor.

"Are you in town for the conference?" asks the woman.

"No, but I like meeting new people. That's all a conference is, anyway. A chance to meet."

"The shaking of hands and the reading of name tags."

"After so many meetings, you still drink at the bar alone?"

"Are you going to leave me here?"

"I'll be leaving here at some point," I say. "Whether you are left is up to you."

She smiles and sips her drink. I have already finished mine, which makes it not much better than a shot. The bartender offers me another. I order bourbon instead. *Whiskey in a glass*, I call it. No mixer, no ice. The smell stings. The sting is like a toothpick slid between the teeth, a mixture of pain and pleasure and the promise of release. I take a toothpick from a bin on the bar. It is plastic and shaped like a sword. It is not designed to pick teeth but to garnish martinis. To slay tiny pirates. I slide the tooth-sword into my drink. I count twenty different types of whiskey behind the bar.

"My name is Natalie," says the woman.

I do not respond with my own name. Like an ancient fairytale, tonight my name is the source of my power, and to reveal it after only one drink would be irresponsible. That's the kind of information that is blurted out only at the end of the night, drunkenly, to the shock and embarrassment of all. I am a little disappointed to know Natalie's name. It came too easily. She tilts toward me. Drooping neckline. A small slice of shadow.

"I like this hotel," I say.

"I like to watch people pass by in the lobby," she says. "They all have a look of disorientation."

"This place, the hotel, is their temporary home, but they recognize nothing of home in it."

"Sometimes you see a frequent traveler, one who moves through the lobby with confidence."

"He has seen this lobby and a thousand like it."

Natalie touches my hand. "You have that same look. One of unflappable familiarity. Have you been here before?"

"I never visit the same hotel twice."

"Do you want to go up to your room?"

"I don't have a room here. Your room?"

"I don't have a room, either."

"The lobby, at least, is ours."

She wraps her fingers around my hand and pulls me from the bar. I follow a step behind, like a child being led through a department store by his mother. We pass the elevator. It dings. Four men step off. They wear blazers with elbow patches and khaki pants and shirts unbuttoned too low. The white hair on their chests pokes out. One of them winks at me. He remembers his own youthful trips to hotels. The women he left hotel bars with. Somewhere an old wrinkled wife waits for him. I think fondly of her wrinkles, their depth a sign of permanence. I do not think of them for long. The smooth flesh pressed to my hand is of more immediate importance.

Natalie leads me into the men's room. Bottles of cologne and lotion are lined up on the counter, arranged by color. Sixteen bottles, from red to blue. They all contain substances scented like flowers so the bathroom smells of a distant garden. An old blind man sits by the sink. He is dressed sharply in a tuxedo and wears obsidian black sunglasses that reflect back nearby images as if from the void of space. His face is round with protruding jowls. His breaths come out raspy, as does his voice.

"Go ahead," he says, "all the stalls are free."

Natalie leaves me for a moment and takes the blind man's hand in both of hers. She lifts it to her mouth. She plants a light kiss there, on the back, the skin drawn and papery. I can see through the skin to his tendons. His arteries and veins. The shapes of the tiny bones inside. There are twenty-seven of them. Natalie comes back to me and takes my hand. In it I see none of those same components.

Natalie opens the first stall. It is less like a stall and more like a walk-in closet, walled from ceiling to floor and sealed with a slatted door. I count fifty-four slats. There is a toilet inside. Thick quilted toilet paper spins on a brass dispenser. Above the toilet hangs a print of a generic landscape. We move to the second stall, the third. Each one Natalie opens reveals a similar setup. It isn't until after she opens the fifth door that I begin to wonder. She is searching for something. The row of stall doors stretches indefinitely into the distance. I can see at least forty stalls, and I don't doubt that there are more beyond my perception. Each looks like the same door set in the same floral-papered wall. There is no mark, scratch, or smudge to distinguish one from the next.

We inspect several dozen stalls, not stopping at any of them. Air-conditioned mist puffs from the vents. I shiver. Natalie wraps her arms around me and hugs me like she would a brother. Like a brother she has not seen in a very long time. I appreciate the warmth of her body, but I do not like feeling like family. My thoughts, until this moment, have focused on the shadow between her breasts. This new familiarity, this comfort, is uncomfortable. I pull away. She smiles and slides her hand down my chest in a way that is not sisterly.

She opens the next stall. It is the forty-seventh. I have been counting.

"Through here," says Natalie.

This stall is not like the others. It is not a stall at all, but a hallway. I cannot tell how long it is. It is long enough to be a hallway and not a stall. I step inside and Natalie follows. The walls are hung with photographs. Each is a picture of me. None of the frames match, different sizes and shapes, materials and moldings. In each picture I am sitting in a hotel lobby. The first is of me as a child. I sit in an overstuffed chair, which looks ready to swallow my tiny body. I am five years old. I remember that lobby. I remember the number of people there. Twenty-seven.

The photographs are arranged chronologically. As I walk deeper into the hallway, I move forward through time, seeing in frozen black and white each and every lobby I have known. I don't know how many photographs there are. Lobbies are maybe the one thing I have never counted. They exist one at a time. It is only now, counting the pictures, that I begin to realize the vastness of their number.

In the photographs, the chairs on which I sit change. From squat and contemporary to ornate and wingbacked. Sometimes just a stool. How often does one consider the variety of chairs? The background in each picture is different: bare walls or picture windows or the blur of distant objects. The only consistency is my expression. I am observing. I am counting.

We have passed many of the photographs before I notice the small brass plates beneath them. On each plate is a number. I recognize immediately that this is the number of people in each lobby. *7, 16, 32, 5*. The numbers go on and on. I stop looking at the pictures, paying attention only to the brass plates and their numbers. I add them together in my head. I divide the sum by the number of photographs. By the number of lobbies. Natalie follows close behind. She looks at me and not the walls.

Ahead, I can see the end of the hallway and in it a door. Light escapes from the crack underneath. I look at the last picture on the left wall. It is a picture of the hotel lobby that we just left. The plate beneath it reads *12*. This photograph is taken from a wider angle than the others. I bear the same expression, but my gaze, the calculation of my eyes, is directed across the lobby at Natalie. In the picture she is dressed differently, in unassuming clothes with a modest neckline. A sweater slopes down her shoulders. Her skirt flows out and hangs past her knees. The promise of her figure remains, but it is concealed. It is wrapped like a gift. I look at her in person, in the hallway next to me, and she is dressed in the same clothes as in the picture.

There is an empty frame on the right-hand wall. The frame is white and perfectly square. The brass plate below it is etched with a number: *2*. It is the only instance of this number in the hallway. Every other lobby was occupied by several people at least. In my memory there is no lobby so empty. It is contrary to the nature of lobbies. They are a place to meet. A place to converge. And while they are most often passed through, enough people are passing with enough regularity to keep them full. Can anything less be called a lobby? Is two enough?

"Open the door," says Natalie, "move on to the next number."

I open the door. I step through. It is another lobby, small and quaint, like a secluded inn. The furniture is mismatched. I can't see out the windows because they are bright with the sun. There is no one else there. Natalie moves beside me. I count us. We are the only two. I count us again to make sure. I sit on a sofa next to the fireplace. The fire burns low but steady. Natalie sits beside me and leans back against my chest. In my mind I see us in the picture missing from the frame.

The scent of cedar fills the lobby and Natalie, up close, smells like a distant garden. With nothing else to count, I talk to her. Even as the hours accumulate toward night, we continue talking, until, with her head cradled to my chest, we sleep.

To my last question, the answer is yes.

Little Gray Moon

He was a little gray moon. Small enough to be held in the palm of one's hand. But a moon is too heavy for that. He would center his orbit on the object of his attention. He orbited Nancy most of all. That's how she knew the moon was in love with her. She imagined that her head was a planet. She worried which of the craters in the moon's chalky skin counted as eyes. But for all the attention he gave her, he would tolerate none in return. Even a glance, which for Nancy was hard to avoid with the little gray moon always passing in front of her face, sent the poor fellow skittering away. He would find some object, a lamp perhaps, and revolve around it, casting the circle of his shadow across the paisley-papered walls of Nancy's living room. She followed his shadow, turning in place, until dizziness overwhelmed her. She flopped back onto the carpet and watched the ceiling seem to spin, wondering if that was how the little gray moon felt all the time, and realizing that while it was very much like love it was something altogether different.

Extispicy

The men of the 110th Infantry Regiment of the 28th Infantry Division sprinted through the Huertgen Forest, the bowels of Europe. Bowels is a synonym for entrails. Later on, the 28th would be known as the Bloody Bucket Division, but at the moment they were the Keystone Division, having yet to interact with a bucket of any sort and most certainly not one filled with blood. They had abandoned their pursuit of the Nazis, which was OK from a historical perspective, since most historians agree that the Battle of Huertgen Forest was a pretty silly endeavor to begin with, though these men, not yet privy to what would later be called history, hadn't abandoned the idea of chasing Nazis altogether, but were temporarily sidetracked chasing a rabbit.

It wasn't an ordinary rabbit, or so the men of the 110th Infantry Regiment would later tell you, those of them that didn't die. It was a war after all, and the presence of a cute animal such as a rabbit doesn't preclude the fact that soldiers die in battle, which would come later, after the rabbit itself had been killed. For the record, the rabbit was actually killed after the first artillery round was fired, and historians who argue that the slaying of the rabbit is what started the skirmish are misled. But yes, this was not an ordinary rabbit. It was an enchanted rabbit, and that's why the fine men of the 110th Infantry Regiment ran after it through the dark, ancient woods of Europe. There was nothing obviously enchanted about the rabbit, it was just something the men felt in their guts, like if indigestion meant something. Indigestion happens in the gastrointestinal tract, which is also called a person's entrails, though usually only if they are dangling out after some sort of severe trauma. The rabbit had entrails, too. So the soldiers' entrails told them there was something special about this rabbit, and there probably was, though there's no way to prove it now.

The soldiers and the rabbit ahead of them neared the Kall River, and the rabbit slowed, not sure whether it could swim, and less sure that drowning might not be a better fate than being captured by the men who followed it with crazed looks in their eyes, the kind of look a person gets when their guts, or entrails, take over the thinking for them.

Now the focus moves to a single soldier, because he is the one involved in all the important action. We'll call him Jim, because he's dead now and won't protest this obvious fabrication of a name. He was born with a different name, when he popped slimy and gross from the womb, which was a location close to his mother's entrails. Corporal Jim, as his comrades would have called him if that had been his actual rank and name, was near the front of the wave of soldiers as they jumped over the underbrush and dodged around slender black tree trunks, and it was his keen eyes that kept the 110th Infantry Regiment on the trail of the rabbit.

When the rabbit stopped by the river, Jim motioned for the soldiers behind him to stop as well. The rabbit turned around, perhaps because it had not yet been twenty minutes since its last meal, and swimming with food still swirling around in the entrails is a recipe for cramping. The rabbit stared straight into the eyes of Corporal Jim, and the Corporal felt the enchantment of the situation, and enchantment is a distant thud.

But no, it was not enchantment, but artillery fire, and somebody from the middle of the Regiment yelled *incoming!* because that's what they do in war movies. The soldiers all ran to nearby trees and hugged them like they hoped they'd hug their wives and girlfriends if they ever got out of this godawful forest and back to America. When you hug someone you love, your stomach flutters, as if butterflies were in your entrails. In the forest they hugged the trees because the artillery shells would strike the trunks above them sending down great timbers and splinters of wood, and lying flat on the ground was a sure way to get impaled and/or crushed like an insect such as a butterfly under a boot.

Corporal Jim, however, did not hug a tree. He crouched down on one knee, sighted his rifle at the enchanted rabbit, and fired. The rabbit practically exploded, or that's what Jim thought it looked like, which would be the next to the next to the last thought he'd have. Pride swelled in him for a moment, for he knew that he'd deprived the Nazis of the services of the enchanted rabbit. And then the artillery shell arrived. It passed through the forest canopy without so much as rustling a leaf, a near impossibility but believable here because the enchanted rabbit was already dead, its entrails splattered into the cool water of the Kall River. The artillery shell, clear of the canopy, fell straight into the middle of Corporal Jim's hunched back, passed out through his stomach, and lodged in the black, fertile soil below the cover of decaying leaves on the floor of the Huertgen Forest.

In his hands, Corporal Jim held his own entrails, and said to himself, *This is pretty disgusting.*

❖ ❖ ❖

The teacher held a gear in his hand. It was shiny like it had never been used and bronze colored, but it was probably made from something that wasn't bronze. He was explaining mechanical devices to his third-grade class. Jim sat in the back of the room because he was thirty-seven. He felt a little awkward surrounded by all the children, but mechanical devices fascinated him, and that's the price you pay for learning. A diagram on the blackboard (the board was actually green, but still the old name survived the changing of the colors, like a tree is still a tree when the leaves turn to red and orange in the autumn) illustrated the inner workings of the cotton gin, invented by some guy named Eli back before even the much-older-than-the-rest-of-the-class Jim was born, and being older, Jim was in a position to question the practicality of learning the inner workings of something so old because it was surely obsolete by now.

The entrails of industry, the teacher said, waving the gear in front of him like he was twirling an invisible lasso to rope equally invisible cattle. The entrails of cattle are used to make sausage, which is pretty gross to think about. From a corrugated cardboard box sitting on his desk the teacher pulled out a metal device with a crank on the side and a receptacle on top and a horn-shaped protrusion on the other side. *This is a meat grinder*, the teacher said. *Does anybody know what a meat grinder does?* A girl in the front row answered, *It grinds meat.* She was a know-it-all and that's why she sat in the front row. Everyone resented her because she was smart and pretty and the other students felt the resentment deep in their guts, most of all right before lunch when they were already hungry.

A meat grinder grinds meat into foods like ground beef, said the girl. Someone shot a spitball at her, but she didn't notice because it was deflected before impact by her protective shield of self-righteousness. This made the class even more resentful. In a few years the resentment of the boys would give way to more hormonal reactions and their entrails would churn at just the thought of her, but the girls would resent her even more.

Also sausage, said Jim. The whole class looked at him, because they didn't know him and why was this man in the class in the first place and more importantly why was he siding with the girl in the front row with her knowledge and her beauty. Jim felt good to be called beautiful. No one had said that he was beautiful out loud, but the students' diaphragms stopped working when they looked at him and they lost their breath and the room was very quiet without even motion in the air. After a moment the students gasped collectively and their lungs pushed down on their entrails.

Who the hell are you? asked the teacher. Jim realized he had given himself away, and looked for the nearest exit. The door was too far, so he jumped through the closed window in the back of the classroom. Jim fell two stories to the playground below. He landed on his back, and with a snap his rib splintered and poked out of his side. Shattered glass from the window showered across him, and when the smart and pretty girl from the front row looked out the window, Jim's once beautiful face looked very much like bloody ground beef.

That's pretty disgusting, said the smart, pretty girl.

⁂ ⁂ ⁂

Jim opened the freezer and removed a covered dish containing leftovers. He was unsure how long ago they were left over from. Also in the freezer was a fetal pig, though Jim couldn't remember why he had put it there. Maybe it was his roommate's. The fetal pig said, *Dude, that stuff has been in here forever.* Jim nodded. Even if he hadn't agreed he would have nodded. It's difficult and rather pointless to argue with a frozen fetal pig.

He pried the lid off the container. It was frozen on, and finally released with a ripping sound. Inside was some sort of pasta, pink and red and covered with frost. Jim, having once seen his own entrails, was reminded of them again. *This is what entrails look like*, he said to the pig. He showed the contents of the container to the fetal pig in the freezer, but the pig became sullen. Jim put the container in the microwave. Hummmmmm went the microwave.

Sorry about that, said the pig, *but you see I haven't any entrails. As everyone knows, the liver starts developing before the digestive tract and I don't even have that yet. I'm kind of sensitive about it.* The pig turned away and stared at the icy wall of the freezer with the two mounds that would have become eyes if he had been allowed to remain in the womb for even just a few more weeks. The pig thought back fondly on the warmth of the womb and the gurgling sounds of his mother's entrails processing the slop she gobbled up from the trough.

The microwave dinged, and Jim removed the pasta. The noodles were limp and the sauce was stuck together in unappetizing clumps, like maybe what blood clots would look like if they were bigger, but probably not because one is blood and the other marinara.

If only my digestive epithelium layer had been given time to differentiate, said the frozen fetal pig, and even though Jim wasn't quite sure what that meant, he thought it meant about the same thing he was thinking, so he agreed with a precise nod of his head. He stirred the pasta as if to let it cool before eating, but he was actually in the process of finding it inedible.

This is pretty disgusting, said Jim.

⁂ ⁂ ⁂

The stomach of the sheep was slit open with a bronze knife, and the entrails spilled out across the stone floor like spaghetti, because this was in Ancient Rome, which would later become Italy, and that's where spaghetti comes from. Jim picked up the liver and held it close to his face pretending to inspect it. He was a haruspex for Emperor Marcus Ulpius Nerva Traianus, practicing the art of extispicy, a form of divination that involved the study of the entrails of ritually sacrificed animals. Jim was too smart to believe such silly superstitions, but hey, a job is a job.

Jim wound the intestines around and around, hand to elbow, like how one might wind a rope if one were in a situation where rope-winding was required, like mountain climbing. Jim was not climbing mountains. He was buying time to come up with a believable prophecy. It was difficult to lie about what the entrails said, given their limited vocabulary. *Good weather, good crops, fertile women.* His employer, the emperor, looked at him eagerly. Jim kept winding.

He never knew what to do with the intestines, so he laid them in a coil beside the gutted sheep. Perhaps he would make Italian sausage, but he wasn't sure if that had been invented yet, and he himself wasn't the inventing type.

Why don't you just ask me what they mean? asked the dead sheep to the emperor. *After all, the entrails belong to me. Who better to interpret them than the owner?* Jim looked at the intestines and the liver and all the other parts he probably should have learned the names of in third-grade biology, and wondered if at this point they actually belonged to the sheep anymore or had entered the public domain. What claim has a dead sheep to the matter that once comprised the living version of the sheep? He asked this of the emperor. The emperor agreed that the dead sheep probably had no claim to the entrails, and told the sheep to *be silent*, which is a phrase only men in positions of great power can get away with using.

But the sheep, being already dead and so pretty much beyond the jurisdiction of even an emperor, ignored the command. *This guy here doesn't even know what he's talking about*, said the sheep about Jim. *He's making everything up as he goes along.*

The emperor looked at Jim and asked him if this were true, and Jim being honest in most ways said, *Yes, sorry about that.* The emperor looked genuinely sad as he ordered the guards to take Jim away, and later he looked sad seated in the Colosseum as Jim stood lonely in the middle of the arena. The lions were released from their underground cages and even the joyous roar of his people could not cheer this cheerless emperor. A knot grew in his entrails. The gutted sheep beside him offered condolences. *You made the right decision*, said the sheep, but the emperor did not respond.

Ten lions raced at Jim and he ran from them. The lions roared and the crowd in the Colosseum roared and everywhere there was roaring. Jim ran as far as he could, which wasn't far because he soon came to the pit that the lions had been released from. He gazed into the gaping shadow of the pit, wondering if he could clear it with a jump, but unsure of his jumping ability because really how often do you test something like that. Jim turned around and looked the closest lion directly in the eyes, and felt something like enchantment stir in his entrails.

The sad emperor, at the prompting of the dead sheep, gave a thumbs-down signal to the head lion, and the lion said, *Okie-dokie.*

Jim sank to his knees and felt the world swirling around him, though it wasn't actually swirling, but it seems like that is a safe assumption of the reaction of a man facing his mortality. The head lion crouched down on one knee, sighted his rifle at Jim, and fired. Jim's torso practically exploded.

The crowd became silent at the shot, save for the dead sheep, who proclaimed proudly, *In this man's entrails I see a bright and endless future for the Roman Empire!*

The nine lions that had not been anthropomorphized into gun-toting impossibilities now pounced on the body of Jim and ripped the living flesh from his bones, and his entrails were gulped down into their entrails with sick squishing noises.

The emperor turned his head away and covered his eyes with his hand. *That's pretty disgusting.*

Unlearn to Seek

Always go to the beach with a small container. In it you will put the many shark teeth you find. You won't find them at first. After your first trip to the beach, you may return home with the container still empty. Do not be frustrated. Be peaceful. Like the container, empty yourself, so that you are ready to be filled at such a time as is found the thing that fills you.

The container should be small enough to fit in your pocket. It should be easy to open and to reseal. Choose a container made from a material that will be resistant to salt water. Metal will rust, paper will dissolve. Plastic is recommended. Any material will work in a pinch. The point of hunting shark teeth is to find them, not necessarily to keep them. You can even drop them into your pocket, though you will likely lose the smallest ones. Shark teeth come in sizes no bigger than a speck, and can slip through the seam, fall from your person onto the very beach from which a moment before you took them. They will sit there until the next tide. They will be buried again in the sand and the shells. At a point in the far future they will resurface, awaiting a keen and practiced eye. They will hold within themselves the hope of an appropriate container.

Choose a day when the sun is high. This will make your shadow short. Otherwise, elongated before you, the shadow will obscure the beach. Within the darkness, shark teeth will be much more difficult to locate. As you strain your mind to find them, your mind too will be pulled into the darkness. You cannot fight the shadow without being swallowed by it. When your shadow is present, let it fall behind you. Face the sun.

Locate the shell line on the beach. This is the area in which you are most likely to find shark teeth. The shells are revealed in narrow bands as the tide recedes. Sometimes, in the lapping water, you can see shark teeth tumbling with the current. Here, the shell line is renewed with each wave, fresh layers revealed and the old washed away. To begin, it is easier to locate a shell line up the beach, away from the water. Sitting still, abandoned there by the tide, the shark teeth will be easier to find. What was forgotten by the waves waits to be remembered by the seeker.

Do not look for shark teeth. By seeking the object you will find nothing. The shape of the shark tooth is lost amidst the thousands of similar shapes on the beach. It seems every shard of broken shell is triangular, posing as what you seek. But if you look beyond the object, to the traits that make it identifiable as the object, you realize the vast difference between broken shells and shark teeth.

A shark tooth is the shiniest object on the beach. Its enamel glints in sunlight. This will not be easily noticeable, the distinction between tooth and shell subtle. Train your eye to discern differences in brightness. You are looking for a small shiny spot against the sand, amidst the mosaic of the shell line. With patience and practice, the shiny spots will become apparent. Your eyes will learn to pick them out subconsciously. On the sand, a glimmering constellation. A reflection of the night sky.

Shark teeth are black. Once you have spotted a shiny object, look for its color. If it is not black, it is not what you are seeking. This process, too, should be internalized. Shininess and blackness should be observed almost simultaneously. The two separate aspects of the tooth, when parsed and reconstructed by the mind, will allow you to locate shark teeth. The whole is broken into its components and reassembled, and this reassembly is called finding.

From different kinds of sharks come different shapes of teeth. All teeth are black and shiny, but they are not identical. The tiger shark's is short and hooked. The sand tiger's is long and needlelike. Despite their variety, the same process is used to locate each type of tooth. Shape is irrelevant. Sometimes there are objects on the beach that mimic the shine and color of shark teeth, usually stones or certain shells. In these cases familiarity with shape can aid in your search. This knowledge will develop naturally, so you should not concentrate on it. Let the idea of shape come over you, as does the falling of night.

Go to the far end of the beach. This should be an unpopulated area, where the sound of the ocean is greater than the chatter of people. Let the sound fill your ears. Breathe in the scent of the ocean so your lungs too are filled. Empty yourself and let the beach flow into your mind. When you begin, you must concentrate on shininess and blackness. You must force your eyes to be aware of the beach, and you must force your mind to be aware of your eyes. This is how the novice searches, always thinking about the goal.

Walk the beach, consciously searching, for about an hour. Place the teeth you find inside your container. Do not worry if you fail to find any. Do not be frustrated if you are fooled into picking up an object that is not a tooth. Fling false finds into the water. Do so with joy. Let falsity sink away.

The first shark tooth you find will bring excitement. Channel this energy into finding more. It is important to keep looking after the first find. This is true overall and for each time you visit the beach. Your eyes, once they have successfully picked out a shark tooth, are then primed to find more. Your mind holds the memory of the first find, and, if you act quickly, that memory will allow you to search more efficiently. It is not uncommon to find several shark teeth in rapid succession, once the eyes have become familiar with the image of what they seek. It is a process of visual memorization, similar to the ability to recognize a face in a crowd.

Continue to force yourself to look carefully until you begin finding shark teeth without thinking at all. At this point, the learning process is complete. The search has been fully internalized. You will look for shark teeth without looking. You will find them without searching. Conscious effort is what makes one a novice. When the process comes to you instead of you to the process, this is what is called mastery.

Look closely at the shark teeth you have found. Spread them out on the table before you. Sift through them. Arrange them by size, by shape. Arrange them randomly. Place them in rows. Scatter them. Pick a single tooth, one that appeals to you. Note its utility. Note its beauty. Its form gives rise to both attributes. In your mind, reassemble the tooth out of these two attributes, utility and beauty. This is when you will truly see it. This is when a shark tooth is found.

You are now here at the beach with me. You have learned the lessons and practiced the art, and your own container, like mine, overflows with shark teeth. The search has become a formality. It is a habit. It is an excuse. The titles of student and master have been reshaped as if by the tide. They cannot be separated. Everyone is student and master. The two titles are reassembled into the whole person, and this reassembly is called finding.

We walk down the shell line, talking of subjects far from the ocean, beyond the flight of crying gulls. We stop, on occasion, to pick from the sand a shark tooth that one of us has spotted.

UNDERTAKEN

My dog's claws clattered on the stone walkway, a sound like spilling marbles. I let him lead me through the park to a bench that was hidden from the main path by a row of bushes. I sat there almost every evening, listening to the rumble of the city fade. The beat of honked horns came more slowly, the general hum of human life quieted as everyone made it home, went indoors. I could still hear the traffic from the freeway, but that was a constant noise, one that you could forget after a while.

"Nice dog."

She'd snuck up behind me, not soundlessly, but ambient like the breeze or the rustling of leaves. I turned to look at her. Her jawline tapered like a wine glass. She rounded the bench and positioned herself lotus-style next to me.

"He's a mutt," I said.

"Hell, who isn't," she replied.

"Somebody somewhere."

My dog walked over to her, and she scratched him behind the ears.

"My name's Dish," I said.

"And the dog's name is what? Platter? Saucer?"

"Dish is my last name, but it's what everybody calls me."

"You can call me Teaspoon, then."

The name fit. I could imagine her stirring something. She wore baggy, ripped jeans, stained and scuffed. Her hair was pulled into a girlish ponytail, which made her look young, but her eyes gave away her age. There was no wonder in them, just a been-there disinterest.

"What brings you to the park tonight?" I asked.

"Same as your dog, I suppose. Piss break."

"You'll have to fight him for the territory."

"I'll win." She wiggled her thumb at me. "It's an evolutionary imperative."

"Technically, we're supposed to be living in trees."

"This monkey's afraid of heights."

"You don't seem like the frightened type."

Her face shifted to a scowl. "What the hell do you know, *Mr. Dish*?"

"I guess about the same as you do about me."

"Oh, I know all about you. Captain Afraid-of-Failure. In to work early, leave late, like that makes you something special. You've got a big fat 401(k) so you can retire when you're sixty and spend the last years of your life not knowing what the hell to do with yourself. I bet you write a check to some medical charity once every couple months, so when a poor kid dies from cancer it's not on your head. You smile at all the pretty girls, but you never take one back to your place because you wouldn't have the first clue how to get her off, and while it's admirable that you care, your sexless existence is pretty goddamn depressing. So you got this dog instead, because you know what he needs, and there's little chance you'll fail him, and even if you do he's not going to go barking it to everybody just what a colossal fuckup his master is."

The words stung. It's not that she was completely right. She wasn't. But what she said felt like it was true, and somehow that was truer than the truth. I twisted the end of the leash in my hands.

"But is that life?" she asked.

"It's all I've got."

She stood, bent down, and kissed my dog on his forehead.

"Maybe you're already dead," she said.

She moved off into the shadows, dragging her feet through the grass.

⁂

I called in sick to work the next day.

"Dish, is that you?" asked my boss.

"Yes, sir. I'm not feeling well."

"Get better," he said. The end of the word *better* faded out, like he was hanging up before he finished saying it.

I called my secretary.

"Don't worry, Mr. Dish," she said. "I'll take care of everything while you're out."

It was true. She could run the office without me.

I dug a pair of jeans out from the depths of my closet. They were balled up behind a tennis racket with broken strings. I uncrumpled the jeans, but the wrinkles resisted my attempts at smoothing. Another day, I would have ironed. The T-shirt that I pulled off a hanger had little bumps at the shoulders from having hung there for so long.

I grabbed the leash. At the clinking of the clasp my dog came running. I fastened it to his collar, flipped off the lights. All my possessions were thrown into shadow. Who would claim them when I was gone? I thought about emptying out the fridge, but decided I didn't owe anyone that particular courtesy.

We walked out of the apartment building, my dog and I, and headed east around the bay. An old sidewalk curved parallel to the shore, just inside a crumbling road. Derelict warehouses faced the bay, all busted down doors and broken windows. In the water, Yorokobi's Island was as flat and desolate as ever. Flocks of seagulls rose from the island and then settled back down, carving arcs in the ocean breeze. Gentle waves, crested with morning sunlight, lapped against the bones of the rocky shore. The busy sounds of the city faded away and the rushing of the ocean wrapped itself around me.

I paused at the whim of my dog, content to let him sniff every green shoot that poked out from the cracks in the sidewalk. Sometimes, something would clank in a warehouse, a rat or just gravity winning another round against time. My dog's ears would perk up, two fuzzy triangles on top of his head. He'd stare at the warehouse for a minute, until he got bored with it, just like history had. We'd walk on, ours but the latest abandonment.

We came to an old bus stop, covered with graffiti. I sat down to rest my feet. Right at eye level someone had scrawled in black permanent marker, *I was here, I swear.*

And then I must have fallen asleep.

⁂ ⁂ ⁂

"Are you following me around or something?" asked a familiar voice. I heard the first half of the question in a dream, the second as I awoke.

Teaspoon was already next to me on the bench, in the same casual lotus position as before. Her eyes were closed, like she was meditating. She wore the same pair of jeans.

I said, "I was here first."

She opened her eyes and tracked them across the battered face of the nearest warehouse.

"But somebody was here before that," she said.

"And the Indians first of all."

"I believe the proper term is *Native American*."

"But didn't they just cross over in the Ice Age? Isn't every last one of us on this continent a guest of whatever animal was here first?"

"It's not like I gave anybody smallpox and stole their land," she said.

My dog walked over to Teaspoon and received a scratch behind the ears. His eyes were wide and bright.

"He's a good dog," she said.

"Never barks or bites," I said.

"Never spreads smallpox."

"I should hope not."

Teaspoon looked directly into my eyes. I glanced away.

"Anyway," she said, "I figured I should poke my head in and say hi, in case I don't get to see you again."

"Yeah, thanks."

She stood and shuffled off toward the hazy skyline of the city. My dog whimpered quietly at her back.

⁂ ⁂ ⁂

Just past the last warehouse there was a single tiny storefront with a brightly lit sign out front, golden letters shining in a blue background: *Ray's Dry Cleaning*. After miles of the worn out shells of empty buildings, Ray's stood out if only for its upkeep. The windows were wiped to perfect smudgelessness, and the brushed aluminum frames looked almost fluid. The awnings were the same colors as the sign and seemed brand new, like they had been hung just that morning. Perfect white light poured out the windows and onto the street, overpowering the black of the asphalt.

I walked up and looked through the door. My breath condensed on the glass in a perfect circle, obscuring the interior. The handle was cold and numbed my fingertips. A bell tied to the door jangled a lush chord, reverberating like in an empty room.

The bell summoned a giant of a man to the counter. His head nearly touched the fluorescent light fixtures, and his hands hung well below the countertop. The fluorescent light made the giant's skin look blue. Eyes like sparks peered out from his tangled bangs. Behind him on the spinning rack were an infinite number of white dress shirts pressed smooth and shrouded in clear plastic bags. The giant looked me up and down with a neutral expression.

"You ain't got laundry," he said.

I couldn't tell if it was a question or a statement, so I answered, "Nope."

He motioned with his massive hand for me to round the counter and parted the dress shirts, creating a crisp white tunnel to the back of the store. I nodded in thanks as I ducked through, pulling my reluctant dog along by the leash. A warm breeze rushed past me, like the air leading a storm in from the bay, the scent of distant waters sucked up and spat out.

The back of the store had more white dress shirts in piles nearly as tall as the giant. I assumed these shirts had yet to be cleaned, though I couldn't see any stain or wrinkle that would render them unwearable. Standing among the piles was a frail-looking man, skin bleached by age to almost the same stark whiteness as the shirts, but splotched with dark spots and creased deeply where the flesh seemed sucked into itself. He wore a shirt exactly like all the others.

He looked at me, beyond me, inside me, the ashen rings of his eyes floating in soupy yellow sclera. He smiled, all gums. His tongue scampered around his mouth like an animal. He stepped forward.

"I guess you're here to go to heaven," he said, his voice high, almost whiny.

"That's the plan," I answered.

"Are you dead?"

"As best I can tell."

"I've seen deader."

"I'm not trying to compete."

"Well," he said, sweeping his arm in an arc, encompassing all the white shirts and the various apparatus used to maintain their whiteness, "this here's the gates of heaven. If you're dead, I don't see a reason not to let you in."

A door behind him cracked open. Brilliant light gushed out, splashing over everything, until all was as white as the shirts. The room seemed to disappear.

I could feel the light on my face, not as heat, but as peace, like the individual cells of my body were unclenching. I sighed, not really regretting anything, but a sigh seemed appropriate. I reached out my hand.

"Hold on a second," said the old man. "You can't go taking your dog into heaven. It's gotta stay behind."

"He's coming with me," I said.

"What would you need a dog in heaven for? That doesn't even make sense."

I stepped forward, ignoring the old man. Who was he to tell me what my heaven was? But the door slammed shut as if it knew my thoughts, and the old man moved between me and the gleaming golden doorknob.

"Come on, man," he said, "I get one like you every century. Hand me the leash, and we can let you in. Your dog will be fine. We'll even find a nice home for it."

My dog looked tired from the long walk, but his mouth stretched into a grin as he panted. He would be fine if I left him. I believed the old man about that.

"I'm sorry," I said, "to have wasted your time."

The old man's toothless maw gaped.

He said, "All the gifts of heaven await you just beyond this door. You'd turn your back on that?"

I smiled. I turned. I pushed my way back through the hanging shirts, and above the rustle of plastic I heard the old man say, "Well, that was a first."

⁂ ⁂ ⁂

The city glowed indistinct in the distance. Nearby, there was no light. Not even a streetlamp. The stars, I guess, but they gave off just enough to see, not to see *by*. The leash went taut behind me. My dog had curled up on the ground. I tried to rouse him but he stayed there, inert. His only motion came from breathing. One day even that would stop.

I sat beside him then lay back. Up above the stars. That's heaven, I thought, but I'd seen heaven and it was something much brighter than the sky, even in daylight.

Footsteps. The sound of someone sitting. Teaspoon cleared her throat. She was several yards off. I raised my head but couldn't make her out in the dark.

She said, "That was your one chance, you know."

"I know," I said.

"What's next?"

Instead of answering I tried to imagine what it would have been like. I closed my eyes, dimming even the stars.

Sleeping Bears

Tom came into work with ATE TOO MUCH SPANAKOPITA LAST NIGHT written on his forehead. It was always something like that. LEFT DIRTY DISHES IN THE SINK. FORGOT TO TURN OFF THE BATHROOM LIGHT. DIDN'T COMPOST A COMPOSTABLE CUP. I hated Tom. After spending most of my 20s with PREMATURE EJACULATION in black block letters across my own forehead, the innocuousness of Tom's faults seemed like a slap. Even his font was better than mine, simple, elegant letters with a subtle serif. Just once, I would have liked for him to come to work with his bangs dangling. I hated how he could always get away with using gel, the sculpted swoop of his hair like a crown.

Mary wore a red bandanna this morning, pulled down all the way to her eyebrows. She flashed me a guilty smile as she passed my desk. Bandannas weren't an acceptable part of the dress code, but the bosses usually looked the other way. A bandanna was better than FUCKED NORMAN FROM ACCOUNTING, which a casual hair flip had once revealed on the intern's forehead. It got Norman fired, but raised him in my esteem considerably. Mary, sloop-shouldered, eyes usually downcast, didn't seem like the type for such a message, but who knew?

Our office consisted of twin rows of desks down the narrow length of the main room. Executives and middle managers lived through the doors on either side. The restrooms were at the end of the room, directly in front of the desks, like that's where we were headed on a slow-moving train. Even if DROPPED A STINKER didn't emblazon the hung head of Jim as he exited the men's room, we would have known who'd done it. Jim, to his credit, never grew bangs. *Owning up to your faults*, the TV shrinks called it, even as you could see the thick makeup that covered their real foreheads and the obvious fakeness of the text that had been painted over top. Jim's head never said anything particularly shameful, but still, I'd never met someone so willing to look you in the eye. As we left the meeting last Friday, at which Jim had presented the budget report, I heard one exec say to another, "That boy has upper management written all over him." The only thing I'd read on his face, though, was MADE UP THE NUMBERS.

⁂

The desk next to mine had been empty for a couple weeks. Stray computer cables blossomed from a slot in the desktop. Dust-free squares patterned the surface where Post-its had been removed. The chair, black and mesh-backed, was rolled into the corner, angled away, the seat raised as high as it could go. When Jen quit, it hadn't been much of a surprise. She came back from lunch one day with JUST INTERVIEWED WITH THE COMPETITION poorly hidden behind a drape of fine blond hair. A week later she gave her notice, and two weeks after that she was gone.

I'd been with the company long enough to have seen that desk empty any number of times. Before Jen it had been

Veronica, Jack, Beth, Casey, and Stephen. There was one other lady, too, but she hadn't even lasted a week. Data entry isn't for everyone.

About midday the new woman came down the center aisle and dropped a cardboard box on the desk, kicking up a small storm of dust. The woman coughed and waved at the air in front of her face. She looked at me, grinning.

"They didn't tell me I'd need a wet rag for my first day."

She had dark skin, hair cropped short and left natural. Her lips were tinged with violet, just barely.

I opened my top drawer and pulled out a few tissues. She took them and wiped down her desk's surface. Each tissue she used turned from white to gray. She looked around for a trashcan, but somebody had taken the one from her cubicle. I slid my trashcan out. She balled up the tissues and tossed them in from across the aisle.

From the cardboard box she pulled out the regular office supplies: stapler, staple remover, tape dispenser, mug full of pens, a rack for file folders, and a mouse pad that featured an image of a kitten. She set each item on the desk as if rearranging a room she'd lived in for years. The last thing she removed from the box was a snow globe containing a tiny Eiffel Tower. The fake snow inside flurried as she moved the globe around the desk, trying out several spots before settling on the far back corner. She saw me looking at the snow globe, and said, "I've never been to Paris."

She tossed the empty box underneath her desk. Days later I'd notice the box in the same spot. She took a seat in the mesh-back chair. It sank a couple inches under her weight.

The woman stared ahead at the space where eventually there would be a computer monitor, tapping one finger on the desktop. Something about her unsettled me, but I didn't know what. She'd done nothing but simple, expected tasks. She'd been pleasant in our brief interaction. She hadn't introduced herself, but I couldn't fault her that because neither had I. Maybe I just missed the emptiness of the desk beside me. Maybe it had to do with how comfortable she already seemed, like she fit in better after five minutes than I did after five years.

She turned to me. "I'm Lakiesha. Most people call me Lake."

"I'm Gar," I said.

"Short for Garfield?"

I nodded. "Don't know whether my parents had a thing for dead presidents or comic strip cats."

It was a line I used all the time. I held my hand across the aisle. Lake looked down at it as if in evaluation, then gripped it and shook, overfast. Her smile was wide, like her mouth had extra teeth. I found myself smiling back. I only noticed my own expression because it felt unfamiliar, like when a new message spreads across your forehead, before you can check a mirror to know what it says.

I let my eyes drift up from her mouth to her eyes and then higher still. It was almost impossible not to read a new acquaintance's message, especially with someone like Lake, whose whole forehead was exposed. I searched the deep brown skin there for letters, for the geometric discolorations, the arches and spans, but what I found was nothing. Not even the hint of a word. I leaned forward without thinking. The creases on her forehead were like the lines on a blank sheet of paper.

Lake chuckled to herself and turned away.

"Thanks for the tissue," she said.

⁘ ⁘ ⁘

By the end of the week, Lake had a computer and was entering numbers into spreadsheets like the rest of us. We said hello each morning and goodbye when we went home at night. I showed her how to use the copier. Beyond that, though, we'd barely spoken, so I was surprised when she asked me if I wanted to grab a drink after work. I said yes before I even stopped to think if I had other plans. I never had other plans.

She drove us from the office to a downtown bar. Her car was a yellow Corvette, convertible, but she kept the top up. It smelled inside of fresh plastic, the air from the AC vents crisp and clean. The padding of the passenger seat barely depressed under my weight, as if mine was the first ass to rest there. I started to ask her how long she'd had the car, but she gunned the engine and the rumble drowned me out.

She parked at a meter right in front of Quills, one of those shiny bars set in the corner of glass high-rises, the kind of place frequented by business execs and lawyers. There was, in fact, a group of lawyers at a table by the door, drinking imported beer and telling lawyer stories. "We trained him and trained him and trained him," said one lady, "but right when he stands up to enter the plea, his forehead changes to say, I DID IT." There was a round of laughter from the table, accompanied by commiserating head shakes.

We bypassed the host stand and took seats at the bar. Lake ordered us both drinks without asking what I liked. That's how I ended up with my first vodka martini, wet with a twist, though I only half knew what that meant at the time. I sipped and was pleased to discover the drink was better than I'd anticipated. Lake drank from hers with a practiced motion, the stem of the glass pinched familiarly between her fingers.

She seemed to savor the feel of the martini, first in her mouth and then as she swallowed. Her shoulders loosened and a soft smile played on her lips.

After a few seconds with her eyes closed, she opened them and turned to me. She looked at my forehead and smirked.

"What?" I said. "What does it say?"

"AWKWARD AT STARTING CONVERSATIONS."

I looked down at the bar.

"It's alright," she said. "Just drink."

The alcohol was surging straight to my head. Lightness spread through my limbs, the first hints of euphoria. I watched the activity behind me in the mirror over the bar.

"So where are you from?" I asked, looking at her look at me in the mirror.

"See? That's not a bad beginning." She stood up and swiped her drink off the bar. "Be right back."

She strode over to the table of lawyers, interrupting one of them in the middle of another anecdote of the legal profession.

"Taylor, right? From Swift and Taylor?"

The lawyer smiled, then glanced up at her bare forehead and stared.

"I'm a paralegal over at Levy and Strauss," said Lake, "and I swear I know you from somewhere."

"Um," he said. "My bus ads, maybe? I have ads on a lot of the local buses. John Bonn."

"Oh my gosh, that's it! I take the bus to work every day. It's nice to meet you anyway! So sorry to have interrupted."

She turned before John Bonn could reply and walked back to the bar. The lawyers all looked at each other, shrugging one by one, until their conversation resumed.

"Did you know him?" I asked Lake, softly so the lawyers wouldn't overhear.

"If you're asking if I take the bus, no." She said it a little louder than necessary.

When the bartender came by, she ordered another round.

"Oh," she said to the bartender, "John Bonn said to put our drinks on his tab."

⁂ ⁂ ⁂

We'd been at the bar for a couple hours when I felt my face change. There hadn't been much talking. Even when I'd managed to ask one of the regular get-to-know-you questions, Lake's answers were elusive.

Me: Where are you from?

Her: Too many places.

Me: Is this your first job in data entry?

Her: No two jobs are alike.

Me: Read any good books lately?

Her: Has anyone written any good books lately?

I rubbed my forehead. I couldn't feel the letters on the outside, but I could sense them from within. Something short, a single word, large font. I leaned to the side to see myself in the bar mirror. There were two of my faces overlapping. I blinked and focused and merged them into one. The text was gibberish. Then I realized it was backwards in the mirror. I tried to read it from back to front. I tried two more times before I got it. DRUNK.

Lake watched me trying to read myself, and chuckled when I finally figured it out.

"Looks like I need to get you home."

"I can take a taxi."

"Your car is still at the office. What time do you want me to pick you up in the morning?"

"I usually get in at seven thirty."

"Great, I'll pick you up at eight."

⁂ ⁂ ⁂

Even though she'd told me eight, even though my brain felt like wool from the hangover, I was dressed and ready at seven fifteen as usual. I poured the remains of my morning pot of coffee into a red Solo cup and went outside to wait. The concrete of the stoop was still damp with morning dew. Sleepy schoolkids trudged past to the bus stop.

I was still sitting there more than an hour later, which made Lake tardy even by her own standards. A car pulled up out front. It wasn't Lake's Corvette, so I ignored it. The car honked three times. A silver Mercedes, a few model years old from the looks of it, though I'm not one to be able to tell much from the looks of a car. It honked again. I glanced around for whoever it might be honking at. Another set of honks. The noise was too loud for my hangover. The tinted side window rolled down.

"You coming, Gar?" asked a voice from inside.

I leaned down to see the driver. Even looking at her face, it took me a moment to recognize that it was Lake. Where had she gotten this second car?

I willed myself standing and eased down the steps to the car door, which Lake had thrown open from the driver's side. She patted the gray leather seat.

"The seats are air conditioned," she said.

I plopped down. Cool air chilled the fabric of my pants, which had wicked up some of the wet from the stoop. Lake accelerated away from the curb before I had a chance to buckle up.

"How're you feeling?" she asked.

"A little groggy."

"I think the word is hungover."

"Yeah."

"At least that's what your forehead says. HUNGOVER ON A WEEKDAY."

I hadn't even noticed, hadn't thought to read myself in the mirror that morning.

⁘ ⁘ ⁘

The water cooler was situated behind the row of desks, at the opposite end of the office from the restrooms. The coffee maker sat on a rickety rolling cart next to that. On the wall above them hung the announcement board, bare cork that only ever had one thing tacked to it, that OSHA poster about not getting maimed or decapitated on the job but if you do, remember you have rights. Even when freshly brewed, the coffee always tasted stale.

I dribbled water from the cooler into a conical paper cup while Tom talked about his plans for a weekend of canoeing on some river I'd never heard of. Mary listened and nodded at the things he said and seemed actually interested. She'd been wearing that same bandanna almost every day for over a week. Jim poured himself the last of the coffee but didn't start a new pot.

"Last time I went," said Tom, "I paddled right past a bear fishing in the shallows."

When he smiled, Tom's jaw muscles flexed and his chin thrust out. His forehead said, HAD A SECOND GLASS OF

WINE WITH DINNER. I sucked down the rest of my first cone of water and refilled. I left just as Tom's story reached the rapids.

Lake's computer monitor quivered with motion as I approached. Usually, I never look at a coworker's computer. Whatever work someone is or isn't doing at a given moment isn't any business of mine. But her screen was practically convulsing, so it was impossible not to glance.

A porn video stretched across the whole screen, currently on a close-up of conjoined genitals. I froze in place, unable to look away, like I was passing an accident on the freeway. I slid with sideways steps into my pseudo-cubicle (the walls not high enough to hide whatever you were doing—watching porn, for example—from curious eyes), and slowly lowered myself into the seat.

I opened a spreadsheet, entered a couple numbers, but I was distracted again by motion coming from Lake's direction. I couldn't see her monitor anymore; it was Lake herself moving in the same rhythmic fashion, hand slid underneath the waistband of her skirt, knuckles pressing up the fabric, tracing small circles. Her eyes gripped shut, mouth set in a tight line. Little noises like stifled screams escaped with the exhalations from her flared nostrils, noises so soft I wouldn't have heard them at all if I wasn't watching.

Lake gasped and her eyes burst wide open and she curled over in her seat as if overtaken by some sudden, unlocalized pain. She pulled her hand from her skirt and held it up close to her face. The thumb tremored. With her other hand she moused something closed on the monitor, then she slumped back in her chair.

I still stared at her when she looked my way. I thought

to avert my eyes, but it was obvious I'd seen everything. Text started to appear on her forehead, not a complete message. Not even letters, really, just curves and lines without the other curves and lines necessary to complete them. She smiled at me and her forehead cleared.

"Went home alone last night," she said.

As if that explained everything.

"You should try it at work sometime." She pointed at my pants, stretched into a khaki pyramid by a half-formed erection. My first thought was *How'd that get there?* even though the answer was obvious.

Tom's canoeing story must have concluded, because he sauntered between Lake and me, followed a little bit behind by Mary. When they passed, Lake was already facing back to her computer, typing an endless stream of numbers on the keyboard.

⁂

That night, Lake secured us another few rounds of free drinks courtesy of a bachelorette party. The bride-to-be wore a pink sash and a tiara and a necklace made of plastic penises. None of the bridal party seemed particularly pleased to be there. They all glowered at each other, like everyone else was to blame for the bride-to-be not having the best night of her life, like it never occurred to them that the problem might be the penis necklace, that a night out can be wild without being a spectacle.

Lake went over to them, feigning drunkenness, though she was only a few sips into her first drink, and gushed over the beauty of marriage and the exciting times to come and the value of good friends who'd throw such a party. It only took her fifteen minutes to turn the table of scowling bridesmaids into a jubilant, story-sharing, dancing-to-the-shitty-jukebox-selection, tequila-shooting-salt-licking-lime-sucking celebration. When she stood to rejoin me at the bar, they begged her to stay. She pointed at me and used my sad posture as an excuse to be excused, but not before she'd entered a couple names and phone numbers into her cell phone, including the name of the bridesmaid with the open tab.

She sat beside me and said, "Three JEALOUSES, one SAW HIM FIRST, and one I CAN'T BELIEVE IT'S HER BEFORE ME."

"What?" I asked.

She pointed to her own brow. "Foreheads. By the time I was done, though, all of them had flipped to DRUNK or LOOKING FOR A RANDOM HOOKUP. The bride was stuck on COLD FEET, but it's hard to turn someone who's about to make a huge mistake and deep down knows it."

"How do you do it?"

"What, get a whole bridal party drunk?"

"Your face. How do you keep the words from forming?"

"That's just how I was born. A clean slate."

"No it's not. I saw the words there, at least parts of letters. Earlier, when you were . . ."

"Masturbating at my desk?"

"Yeah, that."

She turned to me, searched my face, read my forehead, but didn't seem particularly interested in whatever was written there. She rested her hand atop my hand on the bar. It wasn't a romantic gesture. More like she was consoling me.

She said, "You're supposed to save the hard questions until the third date."

"Date?"

She offered a smirk in answer to my question, then angled her face away from me.

She said, "My mother beat me. Beat me bruised and bloody. She was a religious nut, and she saw the messages not as faults but as sins. And sins deserved punishment, no matter how minor they seemed. SPILLED THE JUICE got me smacked around just as much as CHEATED ON A TEST. Even then I was able to control it somewhat. You can't cheat on a test if your face confesses it in front of the teacher, but I could hold it back, make it wait to show up until later. I always tried to keep everything hidden until I went to bed, but I was still learning. It wasn't until I reached thirteen that I figured it out."

Behind us the volume of the bachelorette party had been steadily increasing. Now there was a round of high-pitched giggles. They'd snared a young man into their circle. He fidgeted in his seat, like he wanted to leave, but the bridesmaids on either side of him kept stroking his arm, the touch a kind of promise.

"Figured what out?" I asked.

"Where the words come from. They're not faults, and they're certainly not sins. They're not even regrets. Nobody's head ever said, WISH I'D ASKED KATIE TO PROM."

"I don't even know a Katie."

"Sloane, Vanessa, Shauna, whatever. The point is, none of those things cause the physiological change. The words come from guilt. And not what we're actually guilty of, but only what we *feel* guilty about."

"That doesn't sound so different from faults to me."

"We've all got a million little inadequacies, Gar."

"I don't think I'm particularly little or inadequate."

She laughed once loudly, and I saw a flicker of text on her forehead, but it was quickly swallowed back up in the dark skin, like watching a blemish heal in time-lapse.

"I'm just saying that if the words came from faults, we'd need huger heads to list them all. Or they'd cycle one every second, too quick to read. The only words that ever appear, though, are about the things we feel real guilt over. It doesn't have to be big guilt. Just whatever we know we could have done differently, but didn't."

"So you don't ever feel guilty?"

"Not often, and when I do, I suppress it until I can rationalize the guilt away."

"That can't be healthy."

"Neither is getting thrown against the wall by your mother."

She smacked her martini glass down on the bar, hard enough that I was afraid it would shatter. The little bit of remaining liquid splashed up the sides, then dripped back down, leaving finger-trails on the glass's surface. She signaled the bartender for a refill, and told him the name of the bridesmaid for the tab.

"The first time I came home from school with a blank face," she said, "my mother was euphoric. She'd purged all the sin out of me. It was like that for weeks, her full of self-righteous joy. I never got beaten again, but that wasn't enough for me. I couldn't stand for her to think it was her victory. Back then, text would still appear when I let down my guard. It wasn't natural yet, keeping it blank, but only one thing ever appeared: I HATE MY MOTHER.

"I hated that message even more than I hated the woman

because it meant I felt guilty about hating her. This was a woman who'd done everything she could to crush my spirit, and for some reason I felt guilty that I didn't love her, that I didn't call her *mommy*, that what I wanted more than anything was to crush her like she'd crushed me. So I did. I crushed her.

"After you learn how to clear your forehead, to sublimate your guilt, it's not a long way to manipulating it. You just have to convince your brain that you feel guilty in such a way that it creates the messages you want. And if you start thinking about yourself in the third person, you can switch "You" for "I" and direct messages at someone else.

"At dinner, my mom would always beam at me, at least at my empty forehead, from across the table. She was so proud it made me sick to my stomach. I forked up a couple grains of rice at a time, a couple beans to make it seem like I was eating. Mom never even noticed all the food left on my plate. One night, her stare was particularly insistent and pious, and I couldn't take it anymore, so I did it. I looked her right in the eye, and flashed YOU ARE A SINNER across my head. Just long enough for her to read, for the shock to spread across her face, for her fork to clatter against the plate.

"After that, any time I caught her looking at me, I flashed a similar message. GOD IS DISPLEASED, HELL AWAITS YOU, THE KINGDOM IS CLOSED TO SINNERS. I would fill up the margin of my notes at school with phrases I could use against her. I got pretty creative, but the one that broke her, and I knew it would, was simple: GOD HATES YOU.

"I had just turned sixteen and three years of tormenting my mother had thinned her to a stick of her former self. The only thing her head said anymore was I AM A SINNER or UNWORTHY, stuff like that. She always wore a headscarf.

Whenever I saw her without it, the white of her hair surprised me. It had been jet black before.

"One day, we stopped at the Christian bookstore on the way home from school. She'd started going there at least once a week, filling our shelves at home with new-bought Bibles. She hung a cross over every door. It was time for a new cross, I guess, because she held one up to show me and asked what I thought, her eyes expectant. It's the only memory of her I have when she appears naïve, innocent. And that's when I put up GOD HATES YOU, and instead of flashing it like I always had, I let it stay, and I glared at her, because whether or not there is a God, the only one who hated her was me.

"Panic, real and true, like she'd just come face to face with the bear that was going to kill her, consumed her features. She screamed, wept, fell to the floor, thrashing and kicking, knocking crosses and ceramic Jesuses from the shelf. The scarf slipped from her head, revealing one word repeated dozens of times in a tiny font: DAMNED.

"When she settled into silent weeping, the staff at the store helped me gather the limp, quivering heap that was my mother into the car and I drove her home. I led her inside, put her to bed, then got back in the car and left. Never looked back."

The bridesmaid came up to close her tab. The rest of the party was funneling out the door, pulling the young man and now one of his friends along with them. The bridesmaid signed the check without reading it, hugged Lake, muttered something slurred and friendly, and then scampered away to catch up with the party.

"So you can make your forehead say anything?" I asked.

"Just about."

"Why keep it blank then? Wouldn't it be easier to have

a simple, fake fault?"

"You think I'm the only one who can do this? I'm just the only one honest enough to keep my face empty rather than printing it with lies."

That was a disturbing thought, that there were other people who could control their faces. I snuck a peek at the bartender's forehead. OVERPOURS FOR CUTE WOMEN seemed legitimate enough, but what would it say if it wasn't?

"Don't let it erode your faith in humanity," Lake said. "Most everyone is on the up-and-up."

"How do you know?"

"It takes a liar . . ."

⁂ ⁂ ⁂

That night before bed I stood in front of the mirror, willing my face to change, to say something other than NOT GOOD ENOUGH, which I'd felt form there while listening to Lake. I searched inside for the source of this guilt. I let my gaze drift to my other features. My nose had a little outward turn just before the tip. My left eye was slightly rounder than the right. My lips parted a bit in the middle, as if I was about to purse them for a whistle. Not a bad-looking face, overall. I could say this like someone observing a stranger, except I realized that even with strangers I always focused on the content of their message, identifying them by the types and severity of their faults. It wasn't them but their guilt that I found beautiful or ugly. I'd reduced something complex to a single, over-simple feature. But there was no simple answer to a person, just a tangle of guts and feelings cinched up in a bag of skin. I'd only been seeing the part that hinted at the tangle, which was the same as seeing nothing at all.

In the mirror, for a moment, the black lines of NOT GOOD ENOUGH lightened to gray, revealing my face underneath. My real face, not just the stuff on its surface.

⁘ ⁘ ⁘

I rolled into work at 8:05, the first time I'd ever been late except for when Lake picked me up. My forehead said, STAYED UP ALL NIGHT, and the rest of me said it too. The skin under my eyes felt heavy. My shirt had received only a cursory tuck, poofing out above the belt. It was a clean shirt, but it seemed to have already gathered a day's worth of wrinkles.

I sipped a cup of shitty office coffee and listened to Tom share another one of his stories by the water cooler, this one about a hiking trip that somehow included another encounter with a bear. His forehead said, RUNNING LATE SO USED THE ELECTRIC RAZOR THIS MORNING. His skin looked as smooth as normal to me. But had I ever really looked at him besides his message? I noticed then the way his front teeth bucked out, lifting his lips into a half-kiss when he closed his mouth. Electric razor or not, the skin of his face bore the pocks and discoloration from an adolescence of severe acne. His eyes, which I'd always taken for blue, were actually gray, almost completely colorless.

Tom caught me inspecting him, and his voice faltered, story broken off midstream. The dimple on his chin looked like the knot on an old rotten tree. His ears flapped out wide from his head. His blond hair was obviously dyed that way.

He cleared his throat to cover the pause in his story, and then resumed, trying to avoid glancing in my direction. But he kept looking over and I was always looking back, searching some new part of his face. On my own face, I let the message change, and for once I knew what it said, because I'd pushed it in that direction: BETTER THINGS TO DO.

When Tom read it, there was another pause, just long enough for me to turn and walk away.

I couldn't hold the new message for long, and it shifted back to something of my brain's own choosing as I made my way down the aisle. Whenever it changed, it tingled, like a warm cloth pressed against the skin. Like a blush starting from the outside. For something that had been happening my whole life, I'd never paid much attention to the way it felt before. It had always been accompanied by the dread of what the message might reveal, the worry stronger than the sensation.

Lake was tapping away on her keyboard. She had a program open on the monitor that I didn't recognize. An endless stream of digits scrolled down the right side of the screen. The rest was filled with other data, a jumble of numbers, green on a black background, like she was using a computer from twenty years ago.

I sat down at my desk but didn't turn on the monitor. A couple more sips from the shitty coffee. I admired the perfect clarity of Lake's forehead as she worked across the aisle. Her face made little motions as she concentrated, a lift of the lower lip, a focused squint. She held her hands above the keyboard, then pecked down her index finger on the enter key with dramatic finality. She leaned back and watched the screen.

"Morning," I said.

She smiled at me. "Sorry, I was concentrating. Didn't notice you come in." She looked at my forehead and spoke a single "hah."

"I'm laughable this morning?"

"Just not a very Gar-like message. SELF-SATISFIED?

What's got you so full of yourself?"

I found a little corner of guilt inside myself and focused on it and channeled it to the surface. A tingle spread across my forehead. The new word emerged: SHOW-OFF.

Lake's eyes widened momentarily, and she sat up straighter in her chair. She laughed, this time for real.

"You're a quick study," she said.

I felt the heat of a blush on my cheeks and the tingle again on my forehead. SELF-SATISFIED was already back.

❖ ❖ ❖

Usually I took lunch right at noon, but since I'd come in late and then dallied for a while after that, I was still at my desk at one. The rest of the room was empty, even the bosses' offices abandoned, everyone filed out to restaurants or the lounge downstairs that we shared with the rest of the building.

In the quiet, my keyboard sounded like machine-gun fire. My stomach grumbled, loud enough that I thought it would shake the conference room windows from their frames. My heart thudded deep inside my ears. Some of my coworkers would wear headphones to drown out the noise of the office. I wanted my own pair now to drown out the silence.

Despite the quiet, Lake snuck up behind me and tapped me on the shoulder. I jumped in my seat and slammed my knees on the underside of the desk. She laughed, a cackle really, and I couldn't help but join her even as I winced away the pain. As her laughing subsided, she rubbed her hand across my back, and then my shoulder, and then down my arm to my hand. She was pulling me up and out of the seat and I was following her, neither of us laughing anymore. She cracked open the door to the supply closet and pulled me inside. The door closed and it was black. I fished around in midair for the cord from the overhead light. By the time I tugged it on, Lake's skirt and panties were already around her ankles.

She undid my belt and button and zipper, hooked her thumbs through the belt loops on each hip, and slid my pants down. Then my boxers. She stroked her fingers down the top of my penis, the mostly unfeeling part, and then squeezed it as if testing a fruit for ripeness. She shoved me back against the rack of office supplies, rattling paper clips and thumbtacks, a struggling wind chime of a sound. The wire shelves dug into my back.

She traced the shape of the letters on my forehead with her fingertip. I felt the message change, and she traced this new one, too. She licked her finger, like she was tasting what she'd touched. She rose up on her toes and licked my message directly. Her tongue felt like when a message changes except on the outside.

Lake adjusted my hips then straddled my legs, the warmth of her inner thighs inching up until she was just so. She lowered herself around me. The position offered her no leverage, even when she gripped the shelves and lifted with her arms. After a few abortive thrusts, I slid myself out of her. I turned her around by the shoulders and bent her over and entered her from behind. We stumbled across the closet, some four-legged, heaving animal, and she braced herself against the shelves on the other side.

As we fucked in the supply closet, the sound of our coworkers returning and resuming their jobs simmered on the other side of the door. I stayed as quiet as I could, but Lake let out a moan whenever she had one in her. Then the moans escaped more frequently, with more primal panic and less control. I ran my hand under her blouse and found her breast and kneaded it, probably too hard, but she just moaned louder. Then she was huffing in air and her whole body shot through with little convulsions. I gasped, because I came then too, though I hadn't really known I was going to, even though it felt huge, like there couldn't be anything left in me. I kept going for a good while after she was obviously already done because I didn't want the feeling to end, and my dick seemed able to stay hard forever.

When I stopped, she straightened herself and turned around and kissed me. It wasn't a romantic kiss, not exactly. The kiss seemed to say *thank you.*

"Jesus," she said. "You should write a book on that."

She pulled in a deep, deliberate breath. I matched my breathing to hers, as if to maintain our rhythm.

I said, "I'm usually worried about coming too soon."

"Goldilocks," she said.

"Is that your new nickname for me?"

"Just right."

She looked around the closet and found a T-shirt with the company logo. She used that to wipe us both down—it was amazing the places little bits of wet had managed to smear—and then tossed the balled-up, cummy shirt in the corner behind stacks of paper that looked like they were left over from the age of ditto machines.

While we dressed, Lake said, "Now comes the real test. Think you can keep your forehead innocent for the rest of the day?"

"I don't feel particularly guilty, if that's what you're asking."

She insisted that we both walk out at the same time. Nobody even looked up from their desk.

⁘ ⁘ ⁘

I managed to pass the afternoon without incriminating myself. It turned out to be pretty easy to maintain a message if it was about something I actually did feel a little guilty about. I used ORDERED A WATER BUT FILLED UP WITH BARQ'S AT THE SODA FOUNTAIN until about 4:00, and then switched to CAME IN LATE BUT PLAN TO LEAVE ON TIME to close out the day. I couldn't blank my face yet, but I could make the message as good as empty.

I snuck a peek at Lake from time to time, but she focused on the screen in front of her, carefully entering figures on the number pad. At 5:00 she was still set on the screen, showing no signs of letting up. I hovered by her desk before I left, waiting for her to notice me.

"Hey, goodnight," I said.

Still, she didn't look up. I started to move away. She rolled her chair into the aisle to block me.

"Meet me in the downstairs lobby at 6:55 tonight. Don't be late. The lobby locks at 7:00."

"What for?" I asked.

"Not *that*, if that's what you're thinking." She lowered her face and raised her eyes and smiled coyly. "Well, maybe that."

Mary looked at us from her cubicle. The message on her face changed to BEING NOSY even as she turned away. It was the first time I'd seen her without the bandanna all week, but I didn't have a chance to read the message that was there before it changed.

⁘ ⁘ ⁘

I got back to the office at 6:45, but sat in my car in the lot. The building, windows unlit, loomed, unrecognizable. When the clock on my dash read 6:53, I shut down the car, cutting off a bad country cover of "Wagon Wheel" on the radio, and wended my way through the surprising number of cars still in the lot. Did people always stay this late? If so, why were all the windows dark? Those with windows in their offices were apparently not the same ones working after hours. Inside, the security guard let me pass without question even though I'd never seen her before. The elevator dinged. Lake was inside. She waved for me to join her.

The door closed, and we accelerated upwards. Lake pulled something out of her purse, a brass nameplate, the kind that sits on the front of a desk. She held it up with both hands at chest level. It said, *Barney Fister, President/CEO*.

"Greetings, Mister Fister," I said. "Nice to meet you."

"Some name, right? I was wandering around and found it in an unlocked office."

"I've never visited another office in this building. Sometimes I forget they're even here."

"What about all the other people? You think they're just coworkers you've never spoken to before?"

"I don't speak to most of the ones I actually *do* know."

I followed her off the elevator and around the corner to the darkened confines of our office, tinged red by the exit sign, the light faint and smoky. The objects in the room, from water cooler to copy machine to the cardboard boxes in the corner, were just black blobs.

Lake stopped at her cubicle and flipped on the monitor, shifting the quality of light in the room. The same unfamiliar program as before, the one with green text on a black field, was running through a series of numbers too fast to follow. A five-figure number in the bottom corner of the screen crept up in the decimal column before flipping over a whole number. Even though they scrolled up the screen too fast to read, I started to recognize the figures. They were the same ones I entered into spreadsheets every day.

"What are you doing?" I asked.

"Skimming. Embezzlement. Defalcation. There are so many good names for it."

I looked at the screen again. The five figures in the corner suddenly seemed more significant.

"That's almost eighty thousand dollars," I said.

"Not bad for a few weeks' work."

"Why are you showing this to me?"

"Because I like you and know you can keep a secret."

Even if her face said something then, I wouldn't have been able to read it in the dark.

I asked, "You're not really in data entry, are you?"

"Nothing personal, Gar, but is that even a career?"

She squinted at my forehead. Her face flinched with an unrecognizable reaction, then she leaned in quick and kissed me on the cheek.

She said, "I take a job like this one, get in the system, skim a few cents off large transactions, shuffle the money around, and eventually deposit it in an account of my own. The best part is I also get a paycheck while I'm doing it."

"Are you done here?"

"After tonight, yes. I'll shut down the program and tomorrow tell the bosses I need to go care for my sick mother. Thanks for the opportunity and all that."

"If you get caught, though . . ."

"What court would ever convict someone without guilt written all over her face?"

I took a step back, into the aisle, toward my own cubicle. It's one thing to learn how to lie, it's another to have something worth lying about.

"Where will you go?" I asked

"Where do you want to go?"

It was a question I'd never really considered. My own possibilities had always seemed limited by my faults, as if my forehead was the wall between where I was and where I wanted to be. I grabbed the top of the cubicle and waggled it back and forth, like I was prying the tab off a soda can.

"Anywhere that's not made up of little boxes," I said.

She stood up and joined me in the aisle. Reaching out, hand held like some saint in a painting, she touched my face, chin to cheek to the orbit around my eye. Then she covered my whole forehead with her palm. I wondered if that's what it felt like for her, the message concealed.

"You know how I blank my face?" she said. "Because I only feel guilty about one thing: leaving my mother. The horrible bitch that she was, I still feel like I did something wrong. But I also feel that I did the completely right thing. So I feel guilty and not guilty at the same time, and they cancel each other out. One erases the other.

"But I never stopped running away. I never had somewhere I was going, but now, when you look at me like you want something, like there's something I have worth wanting, like I don't need to change myself to be wantable, then I feel there's direction to my life. At least there might be."

She lowered her hand. We leaned into each other, pressed our foreheads, tilted faces, parted lips.

The elevator dinged and the doors chirped open. Lake pulled me to the floor in her cubicle and reached up to shut off the monitor. We scuttled back under the desk, squeezing as tight into the corner as we could.

A woman giggled on the elevator. The giggling moved around the corner and into the aisle. A man's voice begged for quiet, but it had no effect. The couple passed us and went into one of the doors on the side of the room.

Lake whispered, "I didn't know the executive offices came furnished with drunk bimbos."

I shushed her. She elbowed me in the ribs.

"Let me shut off the program," she said. "I was hoping for another hundred bucks or so, but one can't be greedy."

She crouch-stood in front of her desk and flipped back on the monitor. It flashed bright enough to notify the whole world that we were there, but nothing came from the office but the continued laughter of the woman. Lake tapped a couple keys and then clicked once with her mouse. The screen gave off less light. She cut the power and darkened it completely.

Right then, a scream came from the office, high and throaty. We'd been spotted.

"Run," I whispered.

Lake and I were up and around the corner when the second scream came, this one somehow muffled, full of real fear, not surprise. It was a kind of scream I'd never heard before. I stopped in front of the elevator and turned back.

"What the hell are you doing?" Lake asked.

"No one's following us."

The screaming had been replaced by a barely audible murmur and a sound like slapping. I walked toward the office, then sprinted. Lake said something behind me, stop, I think, but I wasn't listening. When I reached the door, all I heard were hissed breaths. I pawed at the wall until I found the switch and turned on the light.

Tom straddled Mary on the boss' desk, his hands around her neck, thumbs digging in at the base of her throat. Mary was almost still, her fingers losing their grip on Tom's arms, sliding away. His face jerked toward me, eyes wide and feral, mouth set in a snarl. The text on his forehead, usually so benign, said, I WILL KILL YOU. His face twitched, and I saw his hands loosen just so much. Mary coughed.

I crossed the room in two strides, launching myself into Tom, toppling him off of Mary and off the desk, taking the marble paperweight and the fancy pen set with us. We crashed against the ground, tangled, Tom clawing at my face and neck but not able to find purchase. I scrambled a little bit away. Blood dripped from above Tom's eyebrow. My hand grazed the paperweight. I snatched it and advanced on Tom. He was groggy, moving slow. He tried to grapple, but his hands grabbed air. I brought the paperweight down on his head. He swayed. I slammed the paperweight into his temple. He fell to his side. His limbs moved like he was swimming.

Lake was in the room behind me, helping Mary into a sitting position, saying meaningless but comforting phrases to her, stroking her hair, brushing the bangs out of her teary eyes. Mary's forehead said, I TRUSTED HIM. Lake continued to coo nothings, pulling Mary's head down into a motherly embrace. Her own head showed something then, text forming there, but I couldn't read it from where I was, her skin too dark and the message too faint.

"What does it say?" I asked.

"Behind you," she said.

Tom struggled to his feet, wobbling, eyes searching the corners of the room, reaching out his arms as if to stop the spinning in his head. I grabbed him by his shirt and shoved him up against the window. He barely resisted me. Underneath the blood flowing down his face, a new message formed. MURDERER.

Perfectly banal Tom. The man so loved because he was, when you got right down to it, not very interesting. Because he always did the right thing and he told good stories about run-ins with bears. His head only ever confessed some small indulgence. But all of that was fake. There was no bear. Tom himself was the only animal in the story. I had always hated Tom. But now I hated him for how he'd made me hate him, when he was even guiltier than the rest of us.

I held Tom with one hand while I unlatched the window and swung it open. I teetered him back over the sill. Lake watched me. "Stop," she said. But I didn't.

Tom's senses returned enough to struggle, but he could only slap against my chest. His weak kicks failed to connect.

"Apologize," I said, dipping his head lower. The ground was dark and far enough below to be invisible.

He muttered a slurred, "I'm sorry."

"No," I said, and jabbed my finger into his forehead. "Apologize here."

He looked at me like he didn't understand. I dipped him lower.

"I know you can lie. You can make it say whatever you want. So lie to me. Tell me it was a misunderstanding. Make me believe it like you always have. Apologize."

He blinked three times, deliberately. His message faded from MURDERER to a simple I'M SORRY.

I leaned him out the window farther, and before he even seemed to realize what was happening, before I knew it myself,

I let go. He fell head first. The last thing I knew of Tom was a crack against the ground.

Mary pulled her face out of Lake's shoulder and cast tear-streaked stares around the room. Bruises were already forming on her throat. I wondered if she'd use the bandanna to hide them.

"Where's Tom?" she asked.

"He jumped out the window," I said.

"Is he OK?"

"Let's just say the bear finally got him."

⁂ ⁂ ⁂

Before the police arrived, while Lake comforted Mary in the conference room, I went to our desks and pulled up spreadsheets on the computers. I entered half-figures in the last column, like we'd come in to work late when we heard the scuffle. The chairs I left rolled back and spun.

I walked down the long, dark aisle to the men's room. The light switched on automatically, casting fluorescence across the institutional gray tile. I'd already washed my hands once, after I cleaned the paperweight, but I did it again, all the way up to the elbow. I stared at myself in the mirror. My forehead should have said KILLED TOM. I should have been branded with that fault-guilt forever. But all it said was SKIPPED DINNER. The empty knot in my stomach confirmed that this wasn't an outright lie, but I'd need a stronger alibi for the police. I searched my feelings, and found one thing I did regret about the whole situation, that I hadn't killed Tom earlier, before he'd even had the chance to touch Mary. Not exactly something I'd like to confess, but with the right presentation . . .

The old message faded from my forehead and in its place emerged COULDN'T STOP HIM IN TIME. Let the police assume I wanted to stop him from jumping, not stop him from living. The difference between a hero and a villain is in the context of a verb.

I exited the restroom and found Lake waiting right there.

"Mary wanted to clean up a little bit," she said. "Had mascara streaked all the way down to her chin."

"Is she alright?"

"Still confused, but she's starting to put the pieces together. While we were talking, her face shifted to ACTUALLY LOVED HIM. How about you?"

"Me?"

"You did just push Tom out a window, and the police will be here any second. What will you tell them?"

"I'll tell them the same thing I told Mary. He jumped. Must have been scared of getting caught. Anyway, do you really think the police will investigate it when the guy has a suicide note written on his own face?"

Lake reached over and adjusted the rolled cuff of my sleeve. She looked close at my face, first the eyes, and then up to my message.

"How'd you get so good at lying?"

"Had a good teacher."

A message flickered on her forehead, but never fully formed. The door to the women's restroom swung inward, sweeping sudden brightness into the room, and Mary stepped out. Her face was dark under the eyes and pink on the cheeks, but showed no other sign of the night's trauma.

Through the open office door, through the open window, the first flash of police lights shot their red and blue onto the ceiling. We took Mary to the conference room and waited.

⁂ ⁂ ⁂

We were with the police for over two hours, even after the ambulance took Mary to the hospital. She asked for Lake to come with her, but the police said we had to stay a little longer. Lake promised to visit as soon as we were done.

Several different detectives came in and repeated the same questions. It felt cursory, like they were avoiding going back to their desks more than they were investigating. As soon as they'd read Tom's apology and the message on my own face, they seemed to only go through the motions, spending more effort trying to comfort me than to get information.

"You did the right thing," said one cop. And another, "She'd be dead right now if you two hadn't been here." Another, "He was a bad man, and he got what was coming to him." Another, "You're a hero." After an hour of that I was ready to confess just to make it all stop.

Lake assumed a sad, shaken posture, and answered questions in a quiet voice. She wouldn't look at me, and she shrugged off any praise like a blanket on a warm night. Her forehead filled with a faint message, but I never got a good look at it. When the cops said we could go, Lake stood and left without a word. I tried to catch her at the elevator, but she was already gone.

⁂ ⁂ ⁂

I circled around the scene of Tom's death. The body had been hauled away, leaving just its white-taped outline. A dark blotch marred the gray concrete, spreading away from the shape of the head. I ducked under the police tape, which repeated the phrase CRIME SCENE over and over even though the cops themselves had said the fall wasn't a crime. Had Tom landed on his face or on his back? It was impossible to tell.

Lake, myself, the late Tom. Three liars in one office. Was it coincidence? Fate? Or were there many more like us, several in any crowd? The numbers didn't matter. From now on, I would doubt everything I read. The curse of the liar is to suspect lies from everyone else.

I let my forehead say, I'M SORRY, the same confession I'd forced on Tom, but I didn't mean it. Not at all.

⁂ ⁂ ⁂

Lake didn't come to work for two days. The office was somber. Everyone had loved Tom, loved his stories about run-ins with bears, felt comfortable around him, familiar, simpler. Jim handled the duty of cleaning out Tom's desk. No family, it turned out. No one at the funeral but a few people from the office, and not as many of them as you'd expect. That's what Jim had said. He walked down the aisle between the desks with a cardboard box full of the dead man's possessions. On Jim's forehead it said, KEEPING THE NEWTON'S CRADLE FOR MYSELF.

The next day, Lake returned and retrieved the cardboard box from under her desk, the same box she'd unpacked just a few weeks before. She loaded up her things, plus the monitor, which I'm pretty sure belonged to the company. She set her key card on the center of the empty desk. As she walked into the aisle, box hugged to her chest, she leaned in and whispered, "Supply closet."

When I entered, she was busy stuffing office supplies into every empty space in the box. Printer cartridges, pens, Post-its, a dozen rulers as if somebody needed more than one.

"Hi," she said, still snatching items from the shelves.

"You're leaving," I said.

"I told you it was time."

"Should I come with you?"

"It's up to you."

"Were you going to ask me?"

She set a roll of masking tape on top of the already overflowing box like a beige crown. She straightened herself and looked at me finally.

"I can't trust you anymore."

"You're the one who showed me how to do this."

"I was wrong."

"You don't get to decide what's right for me."

"It was wrong for me. For us. I didn't realize it until too late because there's never been anyone else. This thing we do, before we show a false message, before we lie to anyone else, we have to lie to ourselves. We delude ourselves and then delude ourselves even further in believing that's OK. And maybe it's fine when we're on our own, but what do two liars have to fall back on? What truth? Look at you, even now."

I'd felt my forehead change. I'd willed it to change. Not completely on purpose, but it was no accident.

"What does it say?" I asked.

"EVERYTHING WILL BE ALRIGHT."

I had to laugh at that. And Lake laughed too. There was a moment then when we could have kissed, when we could have repeated our supply closet romp. Everything might have turned out different, but we didn't. Everything was different already.

"Let me help you carry that to your car," I said. I lifted the box without waiting for her to agree. It was several times heavier than I expected.

She kissed me by her Corvette, deep and long, but it was a goodbye, not a see-you-later. Simple and sweet, not a hint of bitterness, no guilt to sully the flavor. The taste of regret.

Lake handed me a bulging envelope, sealed with tape, and told me not to open it until I left work. I said OK even though I knew I wouldn't wait. Later I'd realize that was the only time I actually lied to her, at least out loud.

Back at my desk, I slit open the envelope. Inside was a stack of bills, all hundreds, probably ten-thousand dollars total. Stuck to the first bill, there was a Post-it with a single word written on it: SORRY. More than written, the text was drawn, care given to the lines and the serif at the foot of each R. I wondered if this was her font, if this was what her face said underneath the skin, what it would show if she ever let it.

I relaxed, let my feelings out from the place I'd learned to bottle them. I felt the familiar burn of words forming on my forehead. The same feeling as in my chest. I leaned close to the computer monitor, still switched off, and looked at myself in the dark glass. My forehead was blank, just an expanse of pale, naked skin. I tried to will a message to form, but there was nothing left to say.

My 9/11 Story

1

After 9/11, the artist took to drawing pictures of the Twin Towers in the moment just before the first plane hit. Instead of the plane, however, she substituted different objects. The only rule for what she drew was that it had to contain a person. This felt somehow important to her.

She started with other vehicles, cars and trucks, moving on to buses and trains, cruise ships that weren't much smaller than the Towers themselves. Looking closely at one of the cars, a Volvo, revealed a family inside, singing road songs, blissfully unaware of the sudden stop that awaited them. On a bus, strangers hunched next to each other. One man held up a newspaper like a partition, never turning the page and doubtfully reading. On the deck of a cruise ship, people lay out in bathing suits even though the time of day, the early morning, was wrong for sunning.

The artist progressed through space shuttles and submarines, limousines and motorcycle sidecars, garbage trucks and the Disney World monorail, until she couldn't think of any more vehicles.

Next she drew a port-a-john in the plane's place. Inside, though you couldn't see through the plastic walls, a woman hovered herself over the toilet seat, skirt hiked and bunched in her hands, never letting her flesh graze any surface, the thin stream of urine and the soles of her shoes the only things to connect her to the port-a-john at all. Then there was a closet, ripped right out of the house it came from, the bare wood of the joists exposed, electrical wires dangling. A child hid inside, pressed into the corner, draped by his hanging clothes. In the nonexistent rest of the house, the sound of his parents' yelling, the concerned, persistent yip of their small dog, the slamming of doors.

The artist drew coffins like flocks of birds.

Sleeping bags like swarming insects.

She drew her own apartment, and inside the window, which used to overlook the Towers, she drew herself at her desk drawing that very picture of her apartment.

Without meaning to, the artist gradually let her drawings approach the Tower. The first object to impact, to mark a starburst of shatter on the Tower's silver façade, was a Victorian mansion like the ones in the town where she grew up. Painted pink and cream, the house reminded her of a birthday cake.

Another house collided more deeply, shattering windows and sending down a rain of shards. Next came a Walmart, crumpling like a cardboard box while steel and glass exploded around it. The Chrysler Building met its fate, the art deco top the only part still intact. The Space Needle was completely destroyed. It could have been any building at all.

One time a coal mine, just a huge hunk of rock, tunnels hidden within.

A McDonald's playground, bursting like bright plastic confetti.

Pregnant women, giant-sized and stories tall, rendered in gory splatter.

After months of drawings, the artist ran out of objects that contained people. She'd hurled every vehicle, building, tent, tree house, article of clothing, room, wagon, hut, and hovel. She'd inked caves, tunnels, prison cells, showers, tubes, the undersides of bridges, shipping containers, crates, and cribs. There was only one thing left she hadn't drawn, the one thing she knew she shouldn't: the other Tower.

This collision wasn't like the rest. She let it happen slower, so instead of exploding, the structures mashed, starting at met corners, grinding away. The energy of the collision spent itself at the midpoint, and the two halves aligned. To anyone looking, it seemed like only one Tower standing there, waiting for the second plane.

2

There were several technical difficulties in constructing a skyscraper completely out of pillows, but the architect was adamant and his reputation great enough that no one would openly oppose the plan. When it was finished, the Pillow Tower rose to a thousand feet and contained over a million pillows. No one could go inside, of course, but everyone came just for a look. The most common comment from those who first beheld it: *It makes me feel sleepy.*

When the storm came, the Pillow Tower absorbed the rain and became so heavy it could no longer support itself. It toppled, shedding pillows from all sides across whole city blocks. Even wet, they were just pillows, and no injuries were reported.

3

The children watched the news like everyone else. To the boy, the smoke looked thick and solid, like a black snake slithering out of the hole in the Tower. The girl was younger and had no grasp of the size of what was happening. Everything was exactly as big as it appeared on TV. The Towers could fit easily in her hand.

The games the children played changed after that. First, it was soldiers and terrorists. The boy, brandishing a crooked stick for a gun, made the girl pretend to be a terrorist as he hunted her around the yard. When they played with other children, no one else wanted to be a terrorist, so the girl was always the one being chased, alone by herself. Sometimes the other children called her *Osama*, sometimes nasty phrases they'd heard their parents use. The little girl got good at running and nobody could catch her anymore.

The boy introduced a new game called Towers. He would step up to one of the other children and push them. The trick was to fall with your arms held tight to your sides, though anyone who tried smacked their head against the ground. The boy mastered the game first. He would arch his body like the rocker on a chair, toppling at the lightest push and rolling back from his thigh to shoulder, barely bumping his head.

It took the other children longer, but they figured out the technique, too. The girl, however, refused to play. She thought the way that her brother fell was nothing like the way a tower would. A tower couldn't curl itself. A tower had no head to cushion.

One Saturday after morning cartoons ended, several of the children lingered in the living room, trying to think of something to do. The boy suggested Towers. No one else really wanted to play. The fun of it had been in learning how to fall, and now that everyone could do it, what was the point? *Not everyone can do it*, said the boy, pointing at the girl. The girl said she didn't want to.

Come on, Osama. Are you scared? The way he said it was mean, the ess hissed between his teeth and the final *A* bit off at the end. To the girl, there was a difference between being scared and not liking the game, but she also didn't like being called names. *I'll be the Tower*, she said, and stood upright in the middle of the room.

The boy shoved her, too hard, and instead of simply tipping she lifted off the ground. She kept her body straight and rigid, like she was rodded through with rebar. Her head hit the corner of the coffee table and she lost consciousness.

After that she stopped being able to remember new things. When she wakes up every morning, her last memory is the moment her feet lost contact with the floor, the air the only pressure on her skin.

Acknowledgments

The Bitter Oleander: "Unlearn to Seek";
Black Warrior Review: "Children in Alaska";
The Brooklyn Review: "Gravity Changes";
Caketrain: "A Tinkle Is the Sound of Two Things Meeting but Failing to Merge";
Cold Mountain Review: "The Loneliness of Large Bathrooms";
The Conium Review: "The Eating Habits of Famous Actors" and "Sleeping Bears";
Forklift, Ohio: "My 9/11 Story"
Hotel Amerika: "Cockpuncher";
Outlet Magazine: "This Next Song";
PANK: "Extispicy";
Phoebe: "Little Gray Moon" and "Use Your Spoon";
Pindledyboz: "The Tunnels They Dig";
Quiddity: "Joan Plays Power Ballads with Slightly Revised Lyrics";
Red Bridge Press Anthology of Writing That Risks: "When as Children We Acted Memorably."

Hugs all around for the crew at Seersucker Live: Christopher Berinato, Brian Dean, Joseph Schwartzburt, Erika Jo Brown, B.J. Love, Gino Orlandi, Alexis Orgera, Ariel Felton, and Jenny Dunn.

The coffee is on me at Gallery Espresso, where I sat for untold hours and wrote almost everything in this book.

High fives to the Peacock Guild Writers Salon at the Flannery O'Connor Childhood Home, especially Alison Niebanck, Brennen Arkins, Jessi-Lyn Curry, Christy Hahn, and Paul Byall.

Firm handshakes to those who offered feedback along the way: Ariane Simard, Karen Russell, Aimee Bender, Michael Lowenthal, and the editors of the journals where these stories were first published.

A toast to these other supportive people: Catherine Killingsworth, Thomas Calder, J. R. Saylor, Billie Stirewalt, Aaron Devine, Joni and Chris at The Book Lady Bookstore, Traci Lombardo, Lindsay Chudzik, and Peter Conners and Jenna Fisher at BOA Editions.

Love to the whole family, and to that most significant of others, Stephanie Grimm.

And in memory of Jeremy Mullins and Kirk Lawrence, the two best creative collaborators a person could hope for.

About the Author

Zach Powers splits his time between Savannah, Georgia, and Fairfax, Virginia. His prose has appeared in such journals as *Black Warrior Review*, *The Conium Review*, *Forklift*, *Ohio*, *PANK*, and *Caketrain*. He is the co-founder of the literary arts nonprofit Seersucker Live. His writing for television won an Emmy, and he writes about arts and culture for *Savannah Morning News*. Visit his website at ZachPowers.com.

BOA Editions, Ltd. American Reader Series

No. 1 *Christmas at the Four Corners of the Earth*
Prose by Blaise Cendrars
Translated by Bertrand Mathieu

No. 2 *Pig Notes & Dumb Music: Prose on Poetry*
By William Heyen

No. 3 *After-Images: Autobiographical Sketches*
By W. D. Snodgrass

No. 4 *Walking Light: Memoirs and Essays on Poetry*
By Stephen Dunn

No. 5 *To Sound Like Yourself: Essays on Poetry*
By W. D. Snodgrass

No. 6 *You Alone Are Real to Me: Remembering Rainer Maria Rilke*
By Lou Andreas-Salomé

No. 7 *Breaking the Alabaster Jar: Conversations with Li-Young Lee*
Edited by Earl G. Ingersoll

No. 8 *I Carry A Hammer In My Pocket For Occasions Such As These*
By Anthony Tognazzini

No. 9 *Unlucky Lucky Days*
By Daniel Grandbois

No. 10 *Glass Grapes and Other Stories*
By Martha Ronk

No. 11 *Meat Eaters & Plant Eaters*
By Jessica Treat

No. 12 *On the Winding Stair*
By Joanna Howard

No. 13 *Cradle Book*
By Craig Morgan Teicher

No. 14 *In the Time of the Girls*
By Anne Germanacos

No. 15 *This New and Poisonous Air*
By Adam McOmber

No. 16 *To Assume a Pleasing Shape*
By Joseph Salvatore

No. 17 *The Innocent Party*
By Aimee Parkison

No. 18 *Passwords Primeval: 20 American Poets in Their Own Words*
Interviews by Tony Leuzzi

No. 19 *The Era of Not Quite*
By Douglas Watson

No. 20 *The Winged Seed: A Remembrance*
By Li-Young Lee

No. 21 *Jewelry Box: A Collection of Histories*
By Aurelie Sheehan

No. 22 *The Tao of Humiliation*
By Lee Upton

No. 23 *Bridge*
By Robert Thomas

No. 24 *Reptile House*
By Robin McLean

No. 25 *The Education of a Poker Player*
By James McManus

No. 26 *Remarkable*
By Dinah Cox

No. 27 *Gravity Changes*
By Zach Powers

Colophon

BOA Editions, Ltd., a not-for-profit publisher of poetry and other literary works, fosters readership and appreciation of contemporary literature. By identifying, cultivating, and publishing both new and established poets and selecting authors of unique literary talent, BOA brings high-quality literature to the public. Support for this effort comes from the sale of its publications, grant funding, and private donations.

The publication of this book is made possible, in part,
by the support of the following patrons:

Anonymous
Gwen & Gary Conners
Steven O. Russell & Phyllis Rifkin-Russell

and the kind sponsorship of the following individuals:

June C. Baker
Christopher & DeAnna Cebula
Jere Fletcher
Melissa Hall & Joe Torre, *in memory of Michael Hall*
Sandi Henschel
X.J. & Dorothy M. Kennedy
Jack & Gail Langerak
Boo Poulin
Deborah Ronnen & Sherman Levey
Steven O. Russell & Phyllis Rifkin-Russell